PENGUIN CLASSICS

THE LOST HONOR
OF KATHARINA BLUM

HEINRICH BÖLL was the first German to win the Nobel
Prize in Literature since Thomas Mann in 1929. Born in
Cologne, in 1917, Böll was reared in a liberal Catholic,
pacifist family. Drafted into the Wehrmacht during World
War II, he served on the Russian and French fronts and was
wounded four times before he found himself in an American prison camp. After the war he enrolled at the University
of Cologne, but he dropped out to write about his shatter-
ing experiences as a soldier. His first novel, *The Train Was
on Time*, was published in 1949, and he went on to become
one of the most prolific and important of the postwar German writers. His best-known novels include *Billiards at
Half-past Nine* (1959), *The Clown* (1963), *Group Portrait
with Lady* (1971), *The Lost Honor of Katharina Blum*
(1974), and *The Safety Net* (1979). He was awarded the
Nobel Prize in Literature in 1972. In 1981 he published a
memoir, *What's to Become of the Boy? Or, Something to
Do with Books*. Böll served for several years as the presi-
dent of International PEN and was a leading defender of the
intellectual freedom of writers throughout the world. He
died in June 1985.

LEILA VENNEWITZ has translated several books by
Heinrich Böll, including *The Clown* and *Group Portrait
with Lady*.

KURT ANDERSEN is the author of the award-winning,
bestselling novels *Heyday* and *Turn of the Century*, as
well as an essayist and public radio host. He lives in New
York City.

HEINRICH BÖLL

The Lost Honor of
Katharina Blum

OR:

HOW VIOLENCE DEVELOPS AND
WHERE IT CAN LEAD

Translated by
LEILA VENNEWITZ

Introduction by
KURT ANDERSEN

PENGUIN BOOKS

PENGUIN BOOKS

Published by the Penguin Group
Penguin Group (USA) Inc., 375 Hudson Street,
New York, New York 10014, U.S.A.
Penguin Group (Canada), 90 Eglinton Avenue East, Suite 700, Toronto,
Ontario, Canada M4P 2Y3 (a division of Pearson Penguin Canada Inc.)
Penguin Books Ltd, 80 Strand, London WC2R 0RL, England
Penguin Ireland, 25 St Stephen's Green, Dublin 2,
Ireland (a division of Penguin Books Ltd)
Penguin Group (Australia), 250 Camberwell Road, Camberwell,
Victoria 3124, Australia (a division of Pearson Australia Group Pty Ltd)
Penguin Books India Pvt Ltd, 11 Community Centre,
Panchsheel Park, New Delhi–110 017, India
Penguin Group (NZ), 67 Apollo Drive, Rosedale, North Shore 0632,
New Zealand (a division of Pearson New Zealand Ltd)
Penguin Books (South Africa) (Pty) Ltd, 24 Sturdee Avenue,
Rosebank, Johannesburg 2196, South Africa

Penguin Books Ltd, Registered Offices:
80 Strand, London WC2R 0RL, England

First published in the United States of America by
McGraw-Hill Book Company 1975
Published in Penguin Books 1994
This edition with an introduction by Kurt Andersen published 2009

1   3   5   7   9   10   8   6   4   2

English translation copyright © Heinrich Boll and Leila Vennewitz, 1975
Introduction copyright © Bedoozled, Inc., 2009
All rights reserved

Originally published in German under the title
*Die Verlorene Ehre der Katharina Blum, Oder: Wie Gewalt entstehen
und wohin sie fuhren kann* by Kiepenheuer & Witsch, Cologne.
Copyright © 1974 by Verlag Kiepenheuer & Witsch, Koln.

ISBN 978-0-14-310540-4
CIP data available

Printed in the United States of America
Set in Sabon

Contents

Introduction

When this novel was first published, I was a college soph-omore riveted by news coverage of the young kinapped-heiress-turned-revolutionary-robber Patty Hearst and the only student enrolled in a course on "the literature of revolution" taught by a visiting West German professor. Thus I discovered Heinrich Böll, the great *bien-pensant* voice of West Germany. Upon reading this book now, a third of a century later, my first, very parochial American impulse was to wonder why the United States had never produced any real equivalent to Böll.

Sure, the vast majority of fiction writers (and storytellers and artists in every medium) are men and women of the liberal left, like Böll. But no one in the first rank of Amer-ican literature's Greatest Generation devoted so much of his or her work to depicting and deconstructing contem-porary America from a particular ideological angle, and then extended those politics into real life as a premier spokesperson. Norman Mailer's sheer perversity disquali-fies him. Don DeLillo writes splendid sociopolitical fic-tion (*Americana, White Noise*), but he's nearly Thomas Pynchonesque in his reclusive silence on the issues of the day. Interestingly, it's three women—Joan Didion, Susan Sontag, and Toni Morrison—who probably come closest to being America's Bölls. But despite Didion's laconic, re-alistic novels about contemporary politics and policy (*A Book of Common Prayer, Democracy, The Last Thing He Wanted*), her disinclination to making partisan pronounce-ments is entirely un–Böll-like. None of Susan Sontag's novels are politicized chronicles of the way we live now. And given the mainly historical settings of Toni Morrison's fiction, as well as her tight focus on African Americans and tendency to magical realism (our Günter Grass?), she's no Böll, either. Philip Roth has written plenty of political fiction (*I Married a Communist, The Plot Against America*), but he has never been much for real-world commentary. And in the Roth novel most relevant to this one, *American Pastoral,* he takes an unambiguously horrified view of the violent New Left radicals with whom Böll was a liberal quasi-sympathizer. Indeed, among America's best-known serious novelists who were born between the world wars, a majority made political noise mainly for being *illiberal* after the sixties—Mailer and John Updike (and Roth) as alleged misogynists and/or antifeminists, Saul Bellow and Tom Wolfe as bona fide conservatives. And talent and subject matter and style aside, no younger novelist can emerge as the American Böll because the career slot he occupied— first-class fiction writer as household name and galvanizing national voice—has long since ceased to exist in the United States. "Art is always a good hiding place," Böll said upon accepting the Nobel Prize in Literature in 1973, a year before publishing *The Lost Honor of Katharina Blum,* "for intellectual explosives and social time bombs." Such a declaration by a twenty-first-century novelist, at least in the United States, would be an act of fantastic, self-dramatizing hubris. But back in the day in West Germany it was actually true.

In this country Böll is more famous than any of his individual books, but *Katharina Blum* is surely the best known—thanks in part to its brevity, its straightforwardness, and its publication during that brief moment (circa 1970–85) when educated Americans were obliged to have a passing familiarity with important new non-English-language novels and films. Volker Schlöndorff's movie adaptation, released just after the book's English translation appeared, also helped.

It's no wonder the book instantly became a film. (Actually, two films: It was also the basis for an American TV movie, *The Lost Honor of Kathryn Beck,* starring Marlo Thomas and Kris Kristofferson.) Böll's narrative hops around chronologically to keep things interesting, but the simple story (true love, oppressed heroine, good versus evil) takes place mainly over the course of a few days, and is told in the familiar form of the police procedural—something like *Law & Order: Special Political Victims Unit.* And there's also a venerable cinematic history involving lovable crooks (*The Outlaw, Butch Cassidy and the Sundance Kid*) and officially persecuted innocents (*The Wrong Man, Billy Budd*).

The late critic D. J. Enright, who admired Böll, once wrote that "there are three categories of characters in Böll's fictions: the misused or unlucky near-saint; the rascal, good at heart, given to venial if not commendable misdemeanors; and the unvarnished villain, more commonly a bully or hypocrite, greedy, gross, corrupt, than a monster of evil." And so it is here, in this story set in "a certain city," apparently Cologne, in 1974. Katharina is the misused and unlucky near-saint, a working-class divorcée in her twenties who works as a housekeeper and runs a catering business on the side—a woman the book describes as a "nice, smart, virtually blameless person," "extremely attractive" but "almost prudish, in sexual matters." (The secondary near-saints are her employers, the liberal corporate lawyer Hubert Blorna and his architect wife, Trude.) Katharina happens to attend a Carnival party at her godmother's apartment, where she falls head over heels for Ludwig Götten, a stranger about her age. Ludwig is the book's good-at-heart rascal, and beginning the morning after their twelve-hour affair, Katharina is smeared by police and a hysterically reactionary tabloid newspaper as his coconspirator and longtime lover. The Porsche-driving tabloid reporter on the story, Werner Tötges—*töte* means "kill"—is the book's main villain: a gross, corrupt bully.

Since (*spoiler alert*) Katharina confesses to homicide on the third page of the novel, the unfolding narrative mysteries concern only how much she knew of Ludwig's identity, whether and how she helped him elude capture, to what hideous lengths the tabloid press will go to besmirch her, and the nature of her involvement with Alois Sträubleder, a rich businessman client of Hubert Blorna's. The narrator, although never identified, is no omniscient construct but an actual (fictional) person who knows the principal characters personally. And given lines like these—"Too much is happening in this story. To an embarrassing, almost ungovernable degree, it is almost pregnant with action"—the narrator seems to be a fiction writer . . . maybe, say, Heinrich Böll. The deliberately pedantic subtitle—*How Violence Develops and Where It Can Lead*—promotes the conceit that this is a nonfiction chronicle drawn from police documents and conversations with lawyers involved in the case. And yet for all his just-the-facts approach, the narrator is also an incorrigible ironist, such as when he notes, in an aside about wiretap surveillance, that we all ought to "telephone more often . . . since we can never know *who* may derive pleasure from such a call." By portraying its hero's sudden nightmarish descent with both a smirky casualness and a studious neutrality, the book is reminiscent of an earlier twentieth-century German-language writer: Katharina Blum is something like Böll's social-realist Gregor Samsa or Josef K.

A description of her interrogation by police and prosecutors is typical: "At about 5:00 P.M. she had actually been induced to accept another pot of tea and a sandwich (ham)." Concerning the Böll novel immediately preceding *Katharina Blum*, D. J. Enright wrote, "One difficulty is to establish, whatever the occasion, whether or not Böll is being gratuitously bureaucratic, wantonly tongue-in-cheek, supererogatorily documentary." But is that really a difficulty? He is clearly being all three most of the time, and the effect of those mixed motives is to save this novel from being either a generic fairy tale or overearnest agitprop. And it's simply in the nature of Böll's writerly voice. He was *German,* after all, and he has more than a bit of the detail-crazy precisionist in him—which he knows, and self-consciously mocks, even as he's indulging himself. Consider, for instance, these three sentences near the beginning of his Nobel lecture:

> The table upon which I am writing this is 76.5 cm high, its top is 69.5 by 111 cm.
>
> It has turned legs, a drawer, seems to be seventy to eighty years old, was a possession of a great-aunt of my mother's, who, after her husband had died in a madhouse and she herself had moved into a smaller flat, sold it to her brother, my wife's grandfather. And so, after my wife's grandfather had died, it came into our possession, a despised and rather despicable piece of furniture of no value, knocking around somewhere, no one knows exactly where, until it surfaced during a move and proved to have been damaged by a bomb: somewhere, at some time or other, a piece of shrapnel had bored a hole through its top during the Second World War.

The Lost Honor of Katharina Blum is a very contemporary novel—its ripped-from-the-headlines documentary approach, its liberal-left critique of sinister powers-that-be—but even more striking are its extremely old-fashioned qualities. When the author/narrator addresses the reader directly ("Warning: there is worse to come" or "We now return contritely to the foreground"), the asides seem premodern as much as postmodern. The novel is a moralizing melodrama, with its aforementioned villains and heroes, and also an old-school love story in which the lovemaking is not depicted. Chaste Katharina's faith in romantic destiny—"he was simply the One who was to come, and I would have married and had children with him"—and her victimization both seem downright Victorian. The recherché phrase in the book's title, "lost honor," is Katharina's own, and her act of violence is a spontaneous retaliation for a man's unbearable ungentlemanliness.

Of course, the early-seventies way of describing sweet, old-fashioned Katharina's breaking point would be to say she was "radicalized" by the dehumanizing mob anger incited against her by the military-industrial-media complex. And, indeed, when her protector Hubert Blorna finally starts to make a Molotov cocktail "to throw into the editorial offices of the *News*," his wife, Trude, stops him, calling his impulse "spontaneous petit-bourgeois romantic anarchism." It's accurate, but it's also a joke by Böll on generation-of-'68 yuppies. In this novel Böll doesn't explicitly sympathize with left-wing radicalism—Ludwig's crimes in the end have no apparent political motive—but rather with the good-hearted liberals (the Blornas) and apoliticals (Katharina) tyrannized by the reactionaries.

The novel's cool, fussy, pseudononfictional narrative voice works especially well because it's in such strong counterpoint to the manic fabulism of the newspaper articles and headlines that drive the action. (It's analogous to the comedy that derived, a decade later, from the contrast between the deadpan mock-documentary style of *This Is Spinal Tap* and the over-the-top absurdity of its subject.) There have been other unscrupulously fast-and-loose newspapers in fiction (*The Daily Beast* and *The Daily Brute* in Evelyn Waugh's *Scoop; The City Light* in Tom Wolfe's *Bonfire of the Vanities*) and, even more, in film (*The Front Page, Meet John Doe, Ace in the Hole*), but probably none as powerful or as egregious as *The News* in *Katharina Blum*. By means of screaming front-page headlines (OUTLAW'S SWEETHEART and MURDERER'S MOLL) and grotesque distortions and fabrications, a young woman's dreamy night of love is recast as the prearranged meeting of a sociopathic left-wing Bonnie and Clyde. Hubert Blorna tells a *News* reporter that Katharina is "intelligent, cool, and level-headed," a description rendered in the paper as "ice-cold and calculating." And Blorna's reply

to a *News* reporter about her possible criminality—"I
know that all kinds of people are capable of committing a
crime. . . . Katharina? Out of the question"—becomes
"Katharina is entirely capable of committing a crime."
When Tötges uses a disguise to interview Katharina's
sick mother in her hospital bed, Mrs. Blum's rhetorical
question—"[W]hy did it have to come to this?"—becomes,
in his article, "It was bound to come to this." That's because, the reporter explains, part of his job is "helping
simple people to express themselves more clearly."

Böll's *News*—*Zeitung* in German—is only nominally
fictitious, barely even that. At the beginning of the novel,
he gives his own winkingly disingenuous version of the
standard disclaimer: "The characters and action in this
story are purely fictitious. Should the description of certain journalistic practices result in a resemblance to the
practices of the *Bild-Zeitung*, such resemblance is neither
intentional nor fortuitous, but unavoidable." Europe has
always had its sensationalist, irresponsible "boulevard
press"—what the British and Americans call tabloids—
but Germany's right-wing *Bild-Zeitung* is the modern
apotheosis of the type, given its size and influence. Since
shortly after its founding in 1952 it has been the biggest-
selling newspaper in Europe; its circulation in Germany is
proportionately ten times as large as the largest national
papers in the United States.

Naturally, when the ultra-left-wing Rote Armee Frak-
tion (RAF) formed in 1970 and began its campaign of
political violence, the *Bild-Zeitung* went to town. Popu-
larly known as the Baader-Meinhof Gang, after the names
of two of its leaders, the RAF, led by Ulrike Meinhof, in
May 1970 bombed the Hamburg headquarters of *Bild-
Zeitung*'s parent company and broke Andreas Baader out
of jail, after which the spiral of violence and reaction went
into a mad overdrive that lasted for years.

On the one hand, there was plenty to discomfit West
German liberals and the fair-minded of all political per-
suasions, such as the *Bild-Zeitung*'s demonization of a

university professor accused of lending an apartment to
Baader-Meinhof members in 1970 (the episode that Böll
says inspired *Katharina Blum*), and the government's
1972 "antiradical decrees" banning people with question-
able politics from teaching and other public-sector jobs.
After Böll published an essay in 1972 suggesting that press
coverage of the RAF had made a fair trial for Meinhof
problematic, the *Bild-Zeitung* called him a terrorist fellow
traveler, and police searched one of his homes. Given the
paper's fanatical coverage of Baader-Meinhof, Böll declared, its MO wasn't merely "cryptofascist anymore, not
fascistoid, but naked fascism, agitation, lies and dirt."

On the other hand, the movement comprising Baader-
Meinhof and kindred groups, unlike its small and comparatively ethical Weathermen counterparts in America, posed
a serious threat. According to the West German government at the time, the RAF had twelve hundred members
and six thousand active supporters in a country less than a
third the size of the United States. In just one month in the
spring of 1972, they carried out six bombings—once again
of the *Bild-Zeitung*'s corporate headquarters, of police and
prosecutors' offices, and of two U.S. military installations.
In all, the RAF killed thirty-four people, several of them in
kidnappings and targeted assassinations.

Into the middle of this maelstrom, fifty-six-year-old
Heinrich Böll tossed his stick of social dynamite, *The Lost
Honor of Katharina Blum, Or: How Violence Develops
and Where It Can Lead*. It became a bestseller, and once
more, of course, his political opponents accused him of
being an apologist for terrorism, even though he had been
punctilious in the novel about criticizing antiterrorist hys-
teria rather than defending the politics or tactics of the
Baader-Meinhof Gang. And when RAF members assassi-
nated the highest-ranking judge in West Berlin a few
months after the book came out, Böll condemned the kill-
ing. In response, the imprisoned RAF leaders, including
Baader and Meinhof, issued a statement calling his liberal
bluff: "What else did Böll mean in his *Katharina Blum,* if

not that the shooting of a representative of the ruling power apparatus is morally justifiable?" At last, the right and the far left were in agreement: In his fiction, they both insisted, he had effectively legitimized and even glorified politically correct murder. Nevertheless, in his next novel, *The Safety Net,* Böll stayed with the subjects of left-wing political violence, morally bankrupt Establishment media, and the self-perpetuating cycles of paranoia and security overreach.

A few years ago, the Museum of Modern Art in New York mounted a retrospective of the work of the painter Gerhard Richter—another German cultural god of a certain age for whom the spectacle of the Red Army Faction had been an irresistible subject. The exhibit included Richter's blurry black-and-white-photo–based portraits of Baader and Meinhof. He calls the series "October 18, 1977," after the date on which Baader and two comrades committed suicide in prison. (Meinhof had killed herself in prison in 1976.) There was some predictable *tsk-tsk*ing among conservative American critics over this elegiac depiction of anti-American, anticapitalist guerillas, but given that the MoMA show opened in New York City only a few months after the 9/11 attacks, it was surprising how *little* brouhaha it generated, even in the tabloid *Post,* New York's own *Bild-Zeitung.*

However, America's panicky overreactions to the Al Qaeda attacks—the USA Patriot Act; the warrantless wiretapping; the demonization of public intellectuals such as Susan Sontag; the White House press secretary warning commentators that "you have to be careful what you say"—inevitably brought to mind West Germany's Katharina Blum moment in the 1970s. The fact that three of the 9/11 ringleaders had studied together in Germany—indeed, in Hamburg, where the RAF had bombed the *Bild-Zeitung*'s corporate headquarters—only added to the sense of twisted flashback.

Fortunately for us, back in the late sixties and early seventies, when the United States endured its own minor-league flurry of New Left bombings by William Ayers and company, there was no politicized American tabloid press, no Rupert Murdochian *New York Post,* no Rush Limbaugh, no Fox News. We did get our taste of that kind of willful, damn-the-facts fearmongering during the 2008 presidential election, when Barack Obama's opponents portrayed the candidate as a cryptosocialist Weatherman sleeper agent, a man who dared (in Governor Sarah Palin's phrase) to "pal around with terrorists." These transatlantic then-and-now resonances recall Karl Marx's famous line about history repeating, his crack that "historical facts and personages occur . . . twice . . . the first time as tragedy, the second as farce."

In the links between *Katharina Blum* and twenty-first-century America, however, there's also at least one instance where it was farce the first time and tragedy the second: to read Böll's fictional *Zeitung* screed concerning Katharina's treatment by police—"Can it be denied that our methods of interrogation are too mild? Are we to continue to treat with humanity those who commit inhuman acts?"—one can't help but think of the Bush administration's justifications for its torture of captured Al Qaeda operatives. And so maybe even better in this context than Marx is his American contemporary's take on historical recurrences. "History doesn't repeat itself," Mark Twain is supposed to have said, "but it rhymes."

KURT ANDERSEN

Translator's Acknowledgment

I am deeply grateful to my husband, William Vennewitz, for the patient and knowledgeable assistance he has given me in the translation of this book.

LEILA VENNEWITZ

The characters and action in this story are purely fictitious. Should the description of certain journalistic practices result in a resemblance to the practices of the *Bild-Zeitung*, such resemblance is neither intentional nor fortuitous, but unavoidable.

The Lost Honor of
Katharina Blum

For the following account there are a few minor sources and three major ones; these will be named here at the beginning and not referred to again. Major sources are: the transcripts of the police interrogation; Hubert Blorna (attorney); and Peter Hach (public prosecutor, also high-school and university classmate of Hubert Blorna). It was Hach who—in confidence, needless to say—supplemented the transcripts and reported certain measures taken by the police investigators as well as the results of their inquiries absent from the transcripts: not, we hasten to add, for official purposes but solely for private use. Hach was genuinely affected by the concern and frustration suffered by his friend Blorna, who could find no explanation for the whole affair and yet, "when I come to think about it," found it "not inexplicable, but almost logical." Since the case of Katharina Blum will, in any event, remain more or less fictitious, because of the attitude of the accused and the very awkward position of her defense counsel Blorna, such minor and very human lapses in conduct as those committed by Hach may be not only understandable but forgivable.

The minor sources, some of greater and some of lesser significance, need not be mentioned here, since their respective implication, involvement, relevancy, bias, bewilderment, and testimony will all emerge from this report.

2

If this report—since there is such frequent mention of sources—should at times be felt to be "fluid," we beg the reader's forgiveness: it has been unavoidable. To speak of "sources" and "fluidity" is to preclude all possibility of composition, so perhaps we should instead introduce the concept of "bringing together," of "conduction," a concept that should be clear to anyone who as a child (or even as an adult) has ever played in, beside, or *with* puddles, draining them, linking them by channels, emptying, diverting, and rerouting them until the entire available puddlewater-potential is *brought together* in a collective channel to be diverted onto a different level or perhaps even duly rerouted in orderly fashion into the gutter or drain provided by the local authorities. The sole objective here, therefore, is to effect a kind of drainage. Clearly a due process of order! So whenever this account appears to be in a fluid state in which differences in and adjustments to level play a part, we ask the reader's indulgence, since there will always be stoppages, blockages, siltings, unsuccessful attempts at conduction, and sources "that can never come together," not to mention subterranean streams, and so on, and so on.

3

The first facts to be presented are brutal: on Wednesday, February 20, 1974, on the eve of the traditional opening of Carnival, a young woman of twenty-seven leaves her apartment in a certain city at about 6:45 P.M. to attend a dance at a private home.

Four days later, after a dramatic—there is no getting around the word (and here we have an example of the various levels that permit the stream to flow)—turn of

events, on Sunday evening at almost the same hour (to be
precise, at about 7:04 P.M.) she rings the front door bell
at the home of Walter Moeding, Crime Commissioner,
who is at that moment engaged, for professional rather
than private reasons, in disguising himself as a sheikh, and
she declares to the startled Moeding that at about 12:15
noon that day she shot and killed Werner Tötges, reporter,
in her apartment, and would the Commissioner kindly
give instructions for her front door to be broken down
and the reporter to be "removed"; for her part, she has
spent the hours between 12:15 noon and 7:00 P.M. roam-
ing around town in search of a remorse that she has failed
to find; furthermore, she requests that she be arrested, she
would like to be where her "dear Ludwig" is.

Moeding, to whom the young person is known from
various interrogations and who feels a certain sympathy
toward her, does not doubt her statement for a moment; he drives her in his own car to police headquarters, informs his superior, Chief Crime Commissioner
Beizmenne, of the situation, has the young woman escorted to a cell, and fifteen minutes later meets Beizmenne
outside her front door, where a police commando breaks
down the door and finds the young woman's statement
confirmed.

Let there not be too much talk about blood here, since
only *necessary* differences in level are to be regarded as
inevitable; we would therefore direct the reader to television and the movies and the appropriate musicals and
gruesicals; if there is to be something fluid here, let it not
be blood. Perhaps attention should merely be drawn to
certain color effects: the murdered Tötges was wearing an
improvised sheikh costume concocted from a rather worn
sheet, and the effect of a lot of blood on a lot of white is
well known; a pistol is then sure to act almost like a spray
gun, and since in this instance the costume was made out
of a large *square of white cotton,* modern painting or
stage effects would seem to be more appropriate here than
drainage. So be it. Those are the facts.

4

For a time it was considered not unlikely that Adolf
Schönner, press photographer, who was also found shot
but not until Ash Wednesday, in a wooded area to the
west of the festive city, was likewise a victim of Blum;
later, however, when a certain chronological order had
been established for the course of events, this "proved to
be unfounded." A cab driver stated later that he had
driven Schönner disguised as a sheikh and a young female
person dressed as an Andalusian woman to this very
wood. But Tötges had been shot Sunday noon, whereas
Schönner had not been killed until Tuesday noon. Although it was soon discovered that the murder weapon
found beside Tötges could not possibly be the weapon
with which Schönner was killed, suspicion continued to
rest on Blum for several hours, notably on account of motive. If she could be said to have had grounds for taking
revenge on Tötges, she had at least equal grounds for taking revenge on Schönner. But the police did concede that
Blum was very unlikely to have possessed two weapons. In
committing her crime, Blum had gone to work with a cool
intelligence; when she was asked whether she had shot
Schönner too, her answer took the form of a cryptic question: "Yes, come to think of it, why not him too?" Then,
however, the police gave up suspecting her of Schönner's
murder, especially since her alibi proved on examination
to be virtually watertight. No one who knew Katharina
Blum or who, in the course of the investigation, became
acquainted with her character, doubted that, if she had
murdered Schönner, she would have admitted it without
equivocation. In any event, the cab driver who had driven
the couple to the wood ("I'd be more inclined to describe
it as kind of overgrown bushes," he said) did not recognize Blum from photographs. "Hell," he said, "these cute
kids with their brown hair, between five foot five and five

foot eight, age twenty-four to twenty-seven—there's a million of them during Carnival."

In Schönner's apartment no trace was found of Blum, or of anything pointing to the Andalusian woman. Other press photographers and friends of Schönner's knew only that on Tuesday, around noon, he had left a bar frequented by reporters "with some broad or other."

5

One of the leading Carnival officials, a wine and champagne dealer who took pride in his successful labors to restore Carnival jollity, was manifestly relieved that it was Monday and Wednesday respectively before both deeds became known. "A thing like that, just when the festive season's beginning—and you can forget about the Carnival spirit *and* business. If it gets out that fancy dress is being misused for criminal purposes, the whole mood's done for right there and business is ruined. That sort of thing's a real sacrilege. High spirits and a good time need trust, that's what they're built up on."

6

The *News* behaved somewhat oddly after the murder of two of its journalists. Wild excitement! Headlines. Front page. Special editions. Death notices of gigantic proportions. As if—if there's going to be any shooting in the world at all—the murder of a journalist were something special, more important than the murder of a bank manager, bank employee, or bank robber.

It is necessary to mention this excessive attention paid by the press to the event because it applies not only to the

News: other newspapers also treated the murder of a reporter as something wicked, terrible, well-nigh ceremonial,
one might almost say as a ritual murder. There was even
mention of a "victim of his profession," and, of course, the
News clung tenaciously to the version that Schönner had
also been one of Blum's victims. Even if one is bound to
admit that Tötges would probably not have been shot had
he not been a reporter (but, for example, a shoemaker or
a baker), the attempt should have been made to discover
whether it would not have been more appropriate to speak
of a death that *resulted from* a profession; for an explanation will emerge as to why someone as intelligent and cool-
headed as Blum not only planned the murder but also
carried it out and, at the critical moment—one which she
herself had engineered—not only seized the pistol but put
it to use.

7

Let us proceed at once from this lowest of all levels to
higher planes. Away with the blood. Let the excitement in
the press be forgotten. Katharina Blum's apartment has
meanwhile been cleaned up, the ruined rugs have landed
on the garbage dump, and the furniture has been wiped
and put back in place: all this at the expense and on the
instructions of Blorna as empowered by his friend Hach,
although it is far from certain whether Blorna will be ap-
pointed official custodian.

When all is said and done, in five years this Katharina
Blum has invested seventy thousand marks in cash in a
self-owned apartment worth altogether a hundred thousand marks. Hence—to quote her brother, who is at present serving a minor jail sentence—"there's lots of goodies
worth swiping." But then who would be responsible for
the interest and amortization on the remaining thirty
thousand marks, even if a not inconsiderable increase in

value is taken into account? There would be liabilities as well as assets.

Be that as it may, by now Tötges has been buried (with disproportionate pomp and ceremony, in the opinion of many). Strangely enough, Schönner's death and funeral were accorded less display and attention. Why, one may ask? Because he was not a "victim of his profession" but more likely the victim of a *crime passionnel*? The sheikh costume is in the police vaults, likewise the pistol (an 8mm); only Blorna knows the origin of the pistol, whereas the attempts of the police and the public prosecutor's office to find this out have been fruitless.

8

Inquiries into Blum's activities during the four days in question progressed nicely enough at first, and it was only when attempts were made to gather information about the Sunday that they were brought up short.

On the Wednesday afternoon Blorna personally paid Katharina Blum two full weeks' wages at 280 marks per week, one for the current week, the other for the week to come, since he was leaving that same afternoon for a skiing vacation with his wife. Katharina had not only promised the Blornas, she had positively sworn that she really would take a vacation this time and enjoy herself during Carnival instead of picking up extra work, the way she had in every previous year during the festive season. She had delightedly told the Blornas that she had been invited that evening to a small private dance at the home of her godmother, friend, and confidante, Else Woltersheim, and that she was looking forward to it very much, it had been such a long time since she had had an opportunity to dance. And Mrs. Blorna had said: "Never mind, Katie, when we come back we'll give another party, then you can dance again." For as long as she had been living in the city, i.e., for the past five or six years, Katharina had frequently complained of the lack of opportunity "just to go dancing somewhere." There were, she told the Blornas, those dumps where sex-starved students went looking for a free pickup, then there were those Bohemian-type places that were too wild for her tastes, and as for those church dances, nothing would induce her to go to those.

There was no difficulty in establishing that on Wednesday afternoon Katharina had worked for a further two hours at the home of Mr. and Mrs. Hiepertz, where she sometimes helped out at their request. Since the Hiepertzes were also leaving town during Carnival and going to see their daughter in Lemgo, Katharina had driven the elderly couple to the station in her Volkswagen. Despite the parking problem she had insisted on accompanying them to the platform and carrying their bags. ("Not for the money, oh no, we can't offer a thing for a kindness like that, she would be very hurt," Mrs. Hiepertz explained.)

It was confirmed that the train left at 5:30 P.M. If one was prepared to allow Katharina from five to ten minutes to find her car in the midst of the early Carnival crowds, and a further twenty to twenty-five minutes to reach her suburban apartment, so that she could not have entered it until between 6:00 and 6:15 P.M., not a single minute remained unaccounted for, provided one was fair enough to grant that she must have washed, changed, and had a bite to eat, for by 7:25 P.M. she had already turned up at Miss Woltersheim's party, not in her own car but by streetcar, and she was dressed neither as a Bedouin nor as an Andalusian but merely wore a red carnation in her hair, red stockings and shoes, a high-necked blouse of honey-colored raw silk, and a plain tweed skirt of the same color. It may appear unimportant whether Katharina went to the party in her car or by streetcar, but it must be mentioned here because in the course of the investigation it turned out to be of considerable significance.

9

From the moment she entered the Woltersheim apartment the investigation was facilitated because from 7:25 P.M. onward Katharina was, without realizing it, under police observation. Throughout the entire evening, from 7:30 to 10:00 P.M., before leaving the apartment with him, she had danced "exclusively and fervently," as she later stated, with one Ludwig Götten.

10

We must not forget to pay tribute at this point to Peter Hach, the public prosecutor, for it is he alone whom we have to thank for the information—bordering on police-court gossip—that Commissioner Erwin Beizmenne had the Woltersheim and Blum telephones tapped from the moment Blum left the Woltersheim apartment with Götten. This was done in a manner that may be worth mentioning: in such cases Beizmenne would call up the appropriate superior and say: "I need my little plugs again. Two of them this time."

11

Götten, it seems, made no calls from Katharina's apartment. At least, Hach knew of none. One thing is certain: Katharina's apartment was under strict observation, and when by 10:30 Thursday morning there had been no phone calls and Götten had not left the apartment, Beizmenne was beginning to lose both his patience and his nerve, and a detachment of eight heavily armed police officers broke into the apartment, storming it with the most intensive precautionary measures, searched it, but found no trace of Götten, all they found being Katharina, "looking extremely relaxed, almost happy," standing at her kitchen counter drinking coffee from a large mug and taking a bite from a slice of white bread and butter and honey. She aroused suspicion in that she did not appear surprised but rather quite composed, "not to say triumphant." She was wearing a green cotton housecoat embroidered with daisies, with nothing underneath, and when she was asked by Commissioner Beizmenne ("quite roughly," she said later) what had happened to Götten, she said she didn't know when Ludwig had left the apartment: she had woken up at 9:30 A.M. and he was already gone. "Without saying good-bye?" "Yes."

12

Here we should inquire into a hotly disputed question put by Beizmenne, a question repeated by Hach, withdrawn, repeated again, and again withdrawn. Blorna considers this question important because he believes that, if it was in fact asked, it was from this and only from this that Katharina's bitterness, sense of humiliation, and fury may have stemmed. Since Blorna and his wife describe Katharina as being extremely sensitive, almost prudish, in sexual matters, the mere *possibility* must be considered that Beizmenne might—in fury, too, over the disappearance of Götten, whom he thought he had in his grasp—have asked the controversial question. Beizmenne *allegedly* asked the maddeningly composed Katharina as she leaned against her counter: "Well, did he fuck you?" whereupon Katharina apparently not only blushed but said triumphantly: "No, I wouldn't call it that."

It may be safely assumed that, if Beizmenne *did* ask the question, from that moment on any feelings of trust be-

THE LOST HONOR OF KATHARINA BLUM

tween him and Katharina were out of the question. However, the absence of any relationship of mutual trust
between the two—although there is evidence to show that
Beizmenne, who is said to be "not all that bad," tried to
establish such a relationship—should not be regarded as
conclusive proof that he did in fact ask the fateful question. In any event, Hach, who was present when the apartment was searched, is regarded by his friends and
acquaintances as "sex-starved" and it is quite likely that
such a crude idea occurred to *him* on seeing the extremely
attractive Blum girl leaning so casually against her counter,
and that he would have liked to ask her that very question
or perform the crudely specified activity with her.

13

The apartment was then thoroughly searched, and a few
objects were confiscated, notably anything in writing.
Katharina Blum was permitted to get dressed in the bathroom in the presence of a woman police officer by the
name of Pletzer. Even so, the bathroom door had to remain slightly ajar and was kept under the close scrutiny
of two armed police officers. Katharina was permitted to
take her handbag with her, and since the possibility of
arrest could not be excluded she was allowed to take
along her night things, toilet articles, and something to
read. Her library consisted of four love stories, three de-
tective novels, plus a biography of Napoleon and one of
Queen Christina of Sweden. All these books emanated
from a book club. Because she kept on asking, "But why,
why, what have I done wrong?" she was finally informed
politely by Pletzer the policewoman that Ludwig Götten
was a wanted man who had been nearly convicted of
bank robbery and was suspected of murder and other
crimes.

14

When, at about 11:25 A.M., Katharina Blum was finally
taken from her apartment for questioning, it was decided
not to handcuff her after all. Beizmenne had been inclined
to insist on handcuffs, but after a brief dialogue between
Policewoman Pletzer and Beizmenne's assistant Moeding
he agreed to waive this. Since that day marked the opening of Carnival, numerous people living in the building
had not gone to work or started out yet for the annual
saturnalian parades, festivities, etc., so that some three
dozen occupants of the ten-story apartment building were
standing around in the lobby wearing topcoats, house-
coats, and bathrobes, and Schönner the press photographer was standing just in front of the elevator when
Katharina Blum, walking between Beizmenne and Moeding, flanked by armed police officers, emerged from the
elevator. She was photographed repeatedly from the front,
from behind, and from the side, and finally—since in
her shame and confusion she kept trying to hide her
face and so got all tangled up with her handbag, toilet
articles, and a plastic bag containing two books and writing materials—with disheveled hair and an angry face.

15

Half an hour later, after her rights had been explained
to her and she had been given a chance to freshen up a
bit, the questioning began in the presence of Beizmenne,
Moeding, Policewoman Pletzer, and the public prosecutors Korten and Hach. The interrogation was recorded:
"My name is Katharina Brettloh, née Blum. I was born
on March 2, 1947, at Gemmelsbroich in the District of
Kuir. My father was Peter Blum, a miner. He died when
I was six, at the age of thirty-seven, of a lung injury received

during the war. After the war my father again worked in a slate quarry and was suspected of suffering from pneumoconiosis. After his death my mother had to fight for her pension because the welfare office and the miners' local could not agree. I had to start doing housework at an early age because my father was often sick, which meant reduced pay, and my mother took on a number of jobs as a cleaning woman. I had no difficulty in school, although even while I was still there I had to do a lot of housework, not only at home but also in the homes of neighbors and others living in the village, where I used to lend a hand at baking, cooking, preserving, and slaughtering. I also did a lot of housework and helped with the harvest.

"After I left school in 1961 my godmother, Else Woltersheim, of Kuir, helped me to obtain a position as a maid at the Gerbers butcher shop in Kuir, where I sometimes had to help out by serving in the store too. With the aid and financial support of my godmother, Miss Woltersheim, I attended a home-economics school at Kuir where my godmother was an instructor and from which I graduated with very good grades. From 1966 to 1967 I worked as housekeeper at the all-day kindergarten attached to the Koeschler Company in neighboring Oftersbroich, and after that I was employed as a domestic aide by Dr. Kluthen, who had a medical practice in Oftersbroich, where I only stayed a year because the doctor was making more and more passes at me and his wife did not like that. I didn't like it myself. It disgusted me.

"In 1968, when I was unemployed for a few weeks and helping my mother in the house and sometimes helping out at meetings and bowling sessions of the Gemmelsbroich Fife & Drum Band, my older brother Kurt introduced me to Wilhelm Brettloh, a textile worker, whom I married a few months later. We lived in Gemmelsbroich, where on weekends when there were a lot of tourists I sometimes helped in the kitchen at Kloog's restaurant, and sometimes as a waitress behind the counter. After six months I already felt an insuperable aversion to my husband. I don't wish to go into details. I left my husband and moved to town. I was divorced as the guilty party on grounds of willful desertion and resumed my maiden name.

"First I lived at Miss Woltersheim's, until after a few weeks I found a position living in as housekeeper and general help in the home of Mr. Fehnern, certified accountant. Mr. Fehnern made it possible for me to attend night school and adult-education courses and to qualify as a certified housekeeper. He was very kind and very generous, and I continued to work for him after I had passed my exams. At the end of 1969 Mr. Fehnern was arrested in connection with substantial tax evasions that had been discovered among large companies for which he had been working. Before he was taken away he handed me an envelope containing three months' salary and asked me to continue looking after things, he would soon be back, he said. I stayed on another month, looked after his employees, who were working in his office under the supervision of tax officials, kept the house clean and the garden tidy, and took care of the laundry. I used to take clean laundry to Mr. Fehnern in the detention jail, and food too, especially Ardennes pâté, which I had learned how to make at the Gerbers butcher shop in Kuir. Later on the office was closed, the house confiscated, and I had to give up my room. Apparently they had found evidence of embezzlement and forgery against Mr. Fehnern, and he was sent to a regular prison, where I continued to visit him. I also wanted to give him back the two months' salary, but he simply would not hear of it. Very soon I found a position with Dr. and Mrs. Blorna, whom I had met through Mr. Fehnern.

"The Blornas live in a house in the new 'South Side' development. Although they offered me a room there, I declined. I longed to be independent at last and to pursue my career more on my own. Dr. and Mrs. Blorna were very gracious to me. Mrs. Blorna—she is a member of a large architectural firm—helped me buy my own apart-

ment in the suburb to the south that was advertised as
'Elegant Riverside Residences.' In their respective capaci-
ties of corporation lawyer and architect, Dr. and Mrs.
Blorna were familiar with the project. With Dr. Blorna I
calculated the financing, interest, and amortization for a
two-room apartment with kitchen and bath on the eighth
floor, and since by then I had been able to save 7,000 marks
and Dr. and Mrs. Blorna guaranteed my bank loan of
30,000 marks, I was soon able to move into my apartment,
early in 1970. At first my minimum monthly payment
amounted to about 1,100 marks, but since Dr. and Mrs.
Blorna deducted nothing for my board, and Mrs. Blorna
even gave me something to take home every night in the
way of food and drink, I could live very economically and
was able to amortize my loan more quickly than had first
been calculated.

"For four years I have been in sole charge of the Blorna
household. My working hours are from seven in the
morning till about four-thirty in the afternoon, when I
have finished the housecleaning and shopping and completed preparations for the evening meal. I also take care
of all the laundry. Between four-thirty and five-thirty I
look after my own apartment and after that usually work
another hour and a half to two hours for the elderly Hiepertz couple. In both homes I am paid extra for work on
Saturdays and Sundays. In my free time I sometimes work
for Kloft's the caterers, or I help out at receptions, parties,
weddings, dances, and so on, usually on my own for a
fixed fee but sometimes commissioned by Kloft's. My
work there consists of job-pricing and general organization, but sometimes I do duty as cook or waitress. My
gross income averages 1,800 to 2,300 marks a month. In
the eyes of the income-tax department I am self-employed.
I pay my taxes and insurance myself. All these things—tax
returns, etc.—are looked after free of charge by Dr. Blorna's office. Since the spring of 1972 I have owned a 1968
Volkswagen which Werner Klormer, a chef employed at

Kloft's, let me have at a good price. It was getting too difficult for me to reach my various places of work by public transportation. With my car I became sufficiently mobile to work at receptions and parties held in hotels farther away."

16

It took from 11:00 A.M. to 12:30 P.M. and, following a one-hour break, from 1:30 to 5:45 P.M. to conclude this part of the interrogation. During the lunch break Katharina Blum refused to accept coffee and a cheese sandwich from the police, nor did earnest and kindly attempts on the part of Policewoman Pletzer and Moeding, Beizmenne's assistant, succeed in altering her attitude. It was clearly impossible for her—as Hach told it—to distinguish between official and personal relations, to understand the necessity for the interrogation. When Beizmenne, who was enjoying his coffee and sandwiches and, collar unbuttoned and tie loosened, not only looked paternal but began to behave paternally, Katharina Blum insisted on being taken back to her cell. It is a matter of record that the two police officers who had been detailed to guard her urged her to accept coffee and sandwiches, but she obstinately shook her head, remained seated on her bunk, smoked a cigarette and, with wrinkled nose and an unmistakable expression, clearly conveyed her disgust at the vomit-spattered toilet in the cell. Later, at the urgings of the policewoman and the two young policemen, she permitted the former to take her pulse, and when this proved to be normal she condescended to have a slice of cake and a cup of tea brought from a nearby café, insisting, however, on paying for them out of her own pocket, although one of the young policemen, the one who had guarded her bathroom door that morning while she was dressing, was

prepared to "treat" her. The opinion of the two policemen
and Mrs. Pletzer on this episode with Katharina Blum: no
sense of humor.

17

The recording of the witness's personal background was
resumed at 1:30 P.M. and continued until 5:45 P.M.
Beizmenne would have been glad to curtail it, but Blum
insisted on every detail, and consent to this was given by
the two public prosecutors. Eventually Beizmenne also
agreed to this procedure—at first reluctantly, later (as-
tutely enough) on account of disclosures relating to the
background, which in his eyes was becoming important.

At about 5:45 P.M. the question of continuing or sus-
pending the interrogation was raised, of whether Blum
should be released or escorted to a cell. At about 5:00 P.M.
she had actually been induced to accept another pot of tea
and a sandwich (ham); furthermore, she consented to
carry on with the interrogation, Beizmenne having promised to release her when it was over.

The next subject was her relationship with Else Woltersheim. She was her godmother, said Katharina Blum, she
had always taken an interest in her, she was a distant
cousin of her mother's; Miss Woltersheim had got in touch
with her as soon as she moved to town.

"I was invited to this private dance on February 20. It
was supposed to take place on the 21st, the beginning of
Carnival, but the date was put forward because Miss
Woltersheim had some professional commitments for that
date. It was the first time I had danced in four years. I
wish to correct that statement: on various occasions, perhaps, two, three or possibly four times, I had danced at
the Blornas after helping out at their parties. At the end
of the evening, when I had finished tidying up and doing

the dishes, when the coffee was served and Dr. Blorna had
taken over the bar, they would call me in and I would
dance in the living room with Dr. Blorna and other guests,
gentlemen with university, business, or political connec-
tions. After a while I was not all that keen to go along
with this idea, and finally I stopped altogether: often the
men had had too much to drink and made advances to
me. To be more precise: ever since I've had my own car I
have declined to join in the dancing. Before that I had to
rely on one of the gentlemen taking me home. Sometimes
I danced with that gentleman"—she pointed to Hach,
who actually blushed—"over there." She was not asked
whether Hach had been among those who made advances
to her.

18

The prolonged nature of the interrogation was explained
by the fact that Katharina Blum was remarkably meticu-
lous in checking the entire wording and in having every
sentence read aloud to her as it was committed to the record. For example, the advances mentioned in the fore-
going paragraph were first recorded as "amorous," the
original wording being that "the gentlemen became amorous," which Katharina Blum indignantly rejected. A regular argument as to definition ensued between her and the
public prosecutors, and between her and Beizmenne, with
Katharina asserting that "becoming amorous" implied
reciprocity whereas "advances" were a one-sided affair,
which they had invariably been. Upon her questioners
observing that surely this wasn't that important and it
would be her fault if the interrogation lasted longer than
usual, she said she would not sign any deposition containing the word "amorous" instead of "advances." For her
the difference was of crucial significance, and one of the
reasons why she had separated from her husband was that

he had never been amorous but had consistently made advances.

Similar arguments ensued over the word "gracious," as applied to the Blornas. The record contained the words "nice to me," Blum insisted on the word "gracious," and when the word "kind" was suggested instead, "gracious" being considered somewhat old-fashioned, she became indignant and declared that "niceness" and "kindness" had nothing to do with "graciousness," and it was with graciousness that she felt the Blornas had always treated her.

19

Meanwhile the occupants of the building had been questioned; most of them had little or nothing to tell about Katharina Blum. They had occasionally met in the elevator and passed the time of day, they knew that the red Volkswagen belonged to her, some had thought she was a private secretary, others that she was a buyer in a department store; she had always been smartly turned out, pleasant, although a bit on the reserved side. Among the occupants of the five other apartments on the eighth floor, where Katharina lived, there were only two who had more detailed information to give. One was the owner of a hairdressing salon, a Mrs. Schmill, the other a retired employee of the electricity works by the name of Ruhwiedel, and the startling thing was that both statements included the assertion that from time to time Katharina had received or brought home a gentleman visitor. Mrs. Schmill maintained that this visitor had come regularly, maybe every two or three weeks, an athletic-looking gentleman of about forty, from an "obviously superior" background, whereas Mr. Ruhwiedel described the visitor as a fairly young fellow who had sometimes entered Miss Blum's apartment alone and sometimes accompanied by Miss Blum. And this, moreover some eight or nine times during the past two years, "those are only the visits I observed—naturally I can't tell you anything about the ones I did not observe."

When Katharina was confronted with these statements later that afternoon and required to make response to them, it was Hach who, even before actually putting the question, tried to make things easy for her by suggesting that these visitors might have been the guests who had occasionally driven her home from the Blornas. Katharina, blushing deeply from humiliation and anger, asked tartly whether it was against the law to receive male visitors, and since she refused to make use of the way out he had so kindly prepared for her, or refused to recognize it as such, Hach told her, also a bit tartly, that she must realize that a very serious case was being examined, i.e., the case of Ludwig Götten, a case that had numerous ramifications and had been occupying the police and the public prosecutor's office for more than a year, so now he was going to ask her whether the visits, which she was evidently not denying, had always been from one and the same person. And at this point Beizmenne intervened roughly, saying: "So you've known Götten for two years!"

Katharina was so taken aback by this remark that she was at a loss for an answer; she merely looked at Beizmenne and shook her head, and the answer she stammered out—a surprisingly mild "No, no, I met him only yesterday"—did not sound very convincing. Upon now being ordered to identify the visitor she shook her head "almost in horror" and refused to give any names.

Here Beizmenne resumed his paternal role and tried to persuade her, saying there was nothing wrong in having a boyfriend who—and here he made a crucial psychological error—rather than making advances had perhaps been amorous with her; after all, she was divorced and no longer bound by marriage vows, and it was not even—third crucial error!—reprehensible for amorousness occasionally to result in certain material benefits. And at this Kath-

arina Blum finally dug in her heels. She refused to make any
further statement and insisted on being taken either home
or to a cell. To the surprise of all those present, Beizmenne,
subdued and weary—by this time it was 8:40 P.M.—said
he would have her taken home by a police officer. But
then, when she had already risen and was gathering up
her handbag, toilet articles, and the plastic bag, he suddenly barked the question at her: "How in the world did
that amorous Ludwig of yours get out of the building last
night? Every entrance, every exit, was guarded—*you* must
have known a way and shown it to him, and I'm going to
get to the bottom of it. Good night!"

20

Moeding, Beizmenne's assistant, who drove Katharina
home, later reported that he was very concerned about the
young woman's condition and feared she might resort to
something desperate: she was absolutely shattered, done
for, and oddly enough it was only in this state that she
had revealed, or maybe developed, a sense of humor. Driving through town with her, he said, he had jokingly asked
her whether it wouldn't have been nice to go somewhere
where they could have had a drink and dance, with no
embarrassment, no ulterior motive, and she had nodded
and said that wouldn't be bad at all, might even be nice,
and then, when they stopped outside her building and he
offered to take her up to her apartment, she had said,
sarcastically: "Hm, better not, I have enough gentlemen
visitors, as you know—but thanks just the same."

Throughout the evening and half the night Moeding
tried to convince Beizmenne that Katharina Blum should
be taken into custody for her own protection, and when
Beizmenne asked him whether he might be in love he said,
No, he just liked her, and she was his own age, and he

didn't believe in Beizmenne's theory of a major conspiracy in which Katharina was involved.

What he did not report, but Blorna was informed of by Miss Woltersheim, was the two pieces of advice Moeding gave Katharina, who did not object to his accompanying her through the lobby as far as the elevator: somewhat risky advice that might have cost him dearly and, moreover, endangered the lives of himself and his colleagues, for what he said to Katharina as they stood by the elevator was: "Don't touch the phone, and don't look at the news tomorrow," from which it was not clear whether he meant the *News* or simply the news.

21

It was at about 3:30 on the afternoon of the same day (Thursday, February 21, 1974) that Blorna was for the first time putting on his skis at his winter resort in preparation for a cross-country run. From this moment on the vacation to which he had been looking forward for so many weeks was ruined. How glorious the walk had been last evening, shortly after their arrival, tramping for two hours through the snow with Trude, then the bottle of wine by the fireside and the deep sleep beside the open window: lingering over their first breakfast, and again lounging on the terrace for a few hours, warmly wrapped up, and just then, at the very moment when he was planning to set out, this fellow from the *News* had turned up and, with no preamble, started quizzing him about Katharina. Did Blorna consider her capable of committing a crime? "What do you mean?" he replied, "I'm an attorney and I know that all kinds of people are capable of committing a crime. What crime are you talking about? Katharina? Out of the question, what in the world gave you that idea? What makes you think such a thing?"

On finally being told that a wanted man was known to have spent the night in Katharina's apartment and that since about eleven that morning she had been the object of intensive questioning, his first thought was to fly home and be by her side, but the fellow from the *News*—did he really look that unsavory, or did Blorna get that impression later?—said, Well, things weren't really as bad as all that and couldn't Dr. Blorna tell him a bit about her character? And when he refused, the fellow told him that was a bad sign and could be misconstrued, for to refuse to comment on her character in a case of this kind—and this was a front-page story—was a clear implication of a bad character, and Blorna, by now furious and irritated in the extreme, said: "Katharina is a very intelligent, cool, level-headed person," and was annoyed because that wasn't true either and nowhere near conveying what he had wanted to say and ought to have said. He had never had anything to do with newspapers, let alone the *News*, and when the fellow drove off again in his Porsche Blorna unfastened his skis and knew he could forget about his vacation. He went upstairs and found Trude lying on the balcony, snugly tucked up and dozing in the sun. He told her what had happened. "Why don't you call her?" she said, and he made three, four, five attempts to reach her by telephone, but each time the operator's voice came back saying "Your party does not answer." He tried again around eleven that night, but again there was no answer. He drank a lot and slept badly.

22

On Friday morning when he appeared for breakfast around 9:30 looking thoroughly out of sorts, Trude held out the *News* to him. Katharina on the front page. Huge photo, huge type.

KATHARINA BLUM,
OUTLAW'S SWEETHEART,
REFUSES INFORMATION
ON MALE VISITORS

Ludwig Götten, the outlaw and murderer who has been
sought by the police for a year and a half, could have
been arrested yesterday if his mistress, Katharina Blum, a
domestic, had not destroyed all traces of him and covered
his escape. It is assumed by the police that the Blum woman
has been involved in the conspiracy for some time. (For
further details see back page: MALE VISITORS.)

On the back page he saw that the News had trans-
formed his statement that Katharina was intelligent, cool,
and level-headed into "ice-cold and calculating," and his
general observations on crime now read that she was "entirely capable of committing a crime."

The pastor of Gemmelsbroich had the following to say: "I
wouldn't put anything past her. Her father was a Communist in disguise, and her mother, whom on compassionate
grounds I employed for a time as a charwoman, stole the
sacramental wine and carried on orgies in the sacristy with
her lovers."

For the last two years the Blum woman has regularly received male visitors. Was her apartment a conspiracy hangout, a gang's headquarters, an arms cache? How did the
27-year-old domestic come by an apartment worth an esti-
mated 110,000 marks? Did she share in the loot from the
bank holdups? The police are pursuing their inquiries. The
office of the public prosecutor is working around the clock.
More details tomorrow. THE News IS ALWAYS WHERE THE
ACTION IS! Complete story in tomorrow's weekend edition.

That afternoon, at the airport, Blorna reconstructed the
swift sequence of events that followed:
10:25: Phone call from Lüding, very worked up, urging

me to return at once and get in touch with Alois, who was equally worked up. Alois, described by Lüding as quite beside himself—since I have never seen him like that I consider it unlikely—at present attending a conference of Christian businessmen at Bad Bedelig where he is the main speaker and has to lead the discussion.

10:40: Call from Katharina asking me whether I had really said what was in the *News*. Glad to be able to set her right and explain what had happened, and she said (as far as I remember) something like: "I believe you, I really do, I know now the way these bastards work. This morning they even ferreted out my mother, who is a very sick woman, as well as Brettloh and some other people." On my asking her where she was she said: "At Else's, and now I have to go back for more questioning."

11:00: Call from Alois, whom for the first time in my life—and I've known him for twenty years—I heard in a state of agitation and alarm. Told me I must return at once to represent him in a very delicate matter, he had to give his paper now, then have lunch with the businessmen, after that lead the discussion, and in the evening attend an informal get-together, but he could be at our place some time between 7:30 and 9:30 and would still have time to drop in at the informal get-together.

11:30: Trude also feels we should leave immediately and stand by Katharina. I can tell from her ironical smile that she already has a theory (probably correct, as always) as to Alois's problems.

12:15: Reservations made, packing done, bill paid. After a vacation lasting barely forty hours, in taxi en route to I. At the airport in I., waited from 2 to 3 P.M. for fog to lift. Long talk with Trude about Katharina, of whom, as Trude knows, I am very, very fond. Also discussed how we had encouraged Katharina not to be so supersensitive but to forget her unhappy childhood and unfortunate marriage. How we had tried to overcome her pride in money matters and to arrange for cheaper credit from our own funds than she could get from the bank. Even when we explained that, if she gave us 9 per cent instead of the 14 per cent she has to pay the bank, we would lose nothing and she would save quite a bit, she was not convinced. How much we owe Katharina! Since she has been running our home in her quiet, pleasant manner, not only have our expenses gone down but the extent to which she has freed us for our professional lives is almost impossible to express in terms of money. She has released us from the chaos that for five years had been weighing so heavily on our marriage and our professional lives.

Decide about 4:30 that the fog doesn't look as if it's going to lift and so to take the train. On Trude's advice I do *not* call Alois Sträubleder. Taxi to station, where we just manage to catch the 5:45 for Frankfurt. Wretched journey—nausea, frayed nerves. Even Trude serious and worried. She has a sense of foreboding. In spite of utter exhaustion changed trains in Munich, managed to get a sleeper. We both anticipate trouble with and over Katharina, problems with Lüding and Sträubleder.

23

Right on Saturday morning, on arriving at the station in the still celebrating city, rumpled and wretched as the couple was: right there on the platform is the *News*, once again with Katharina on the front page, now shown walking down the steps of police headquarters accompanied by a plain-clothes police officer. MURDERER'S MOLL WON'T TALK! NO HINT AS TO GÖTTEN'S WHEREABOUTS! POLICE ON FULL ALERT.

Trude bought the rag, and in silence they took a cab. As he was paying the driver while Trude was opening the front door, the driver pointed to the *News*, saying: "You're in there too, I recognized you right off. You're that broad's attorney, and her boss too, right?" Blorna overtipped the man who, with a grin that seemed less gloating than his tone of voice, carried their bags and skis into the hall and gave them a pleasant "So long now."

Trude had already plugged in the coffee-maker and was washing her hands in the bathroom. The *News* lay on the table in the living room together with two telegrams, one from Lüding and the other from Sträubleder. Lüding's: "Your failure to contact me disappointing to say the least. Lüding." Sträubleder's: "Fail to understand your letting me down like this. Expect immediate call. Alois."

It was just on eight-fifteen, almost the very hour at which Katharina normally served their breakfast: how attractively she always set the table, with flowers, freshly laundered tablecloth and napkins, various kinds of bread, honey, eggs, and coffee, and, for Trude, toast and marmalade.

Even Trude waxed almost sentimental as she brought in the coffee, a few slices of rye crisp, some butter and honey. "It'll never be the same, never. They'll destroy that girl. If not the police, then the *News,* and when the *News* has finished with her it'll be the public. Here, read this first, then phone those gentlemen visitors." He read:

The *News,* in its unceasing efforts to keep its readers fully abreast of events, has been successful in gathering further information throwing light on the character of Blum and her murky past. *News* reporters managed to ascertain the whereabouts of Miss Blum's invalid mother, who began by complaining that her daughter had not been to see her for a long time. Then, when confronted by the irrefutable facts, she said: "It was bound to come to this, it was bound to end like this." Miss Blum's former husband, Wilhelm Brettloh, a respectable textile worker who divorced his wife on grounds of willful desertion, was even more eager to supply the *News* with information: "Now," he said, barely managing to restrain his tears, "now I know why she walked out on me. Why she threw me over. *That's* what was going on. I see it all now. Our modest happiness was not enough for her. She was ambitious, and how is an honest, modest workingman ever to come by a Porsche? Maybe" (he added

sagely) "you can pass my advice along to your readers:
That's how false ideas about socialism are bound to end. I
ask you and your readers: How does a housemaid come by
such wealth? Not honestly, that's for sure. Now I know
why I was always scared by her radical views, her hostility
to the Church, and I bless Our Lord's wisdom in not sending us children. Now when I learn that she prefers the
caresses of a murderer and a thief to my straightforward
affection, that part is explained too. And yet I feel bound to
cry out to her: My little Katharina, if only you had stayed
with me! As the years went by we too would one day have
been able to own a home and a small car, I could hardly
have offered you a Porsche, merely such modest happiness
as can be offered by an honest workingman who doesn't
trust the unions. Ah, Katharina!"

Also on the back page, under the heading "RETIRED
COUPLE HORRIFIED BUT NOT SURPRISED," Blorna found
a column marked in red:

Berthold Hiepertz, retired high-school principal, and his
wife Mrs. Erna Hiepertz, appeared horrified to learn of
Blum's activities but not "especially surprised." In Lemgo
a woman reporter from the News called on the couple at
the home of their married daughter, director of a sanatorium in that town, and Mr. Hiepertz, teacher of classical
languages and history in whose home Blum had worked for
three years, stated: "In every respect a very radical person
who cleverly succeeded in deceiving us."

(Hiepertz, whom Blorna telephoned later, swore that
what he had actually said was: "If Katharina is a radical,
then she is radical in her helpfulness, her organizing ability, and her intelligence—or I am very much mistaken in
her, and I have had forty years' experience as a teacher
and have seldom been deceived.")
(Continued from page 1:)

Miss Blum's former husband, now a completely broken man, on whom the *News* called during a rehearsal by the Gemmelsbroich Fife & Drum Corps, turned aside to conceal his tears. The other corps members, to quote Mr. Meffels, retired farmer, also turned aside in horror from Katharina, who had always acted so strangely and always pretended to be so easily shocked. The innocent Carnival pleasures of an honest workingman might well be said to have been clouded.

And finally a picture of Blorna and Trude, in their garden beside the swimming pool. Caption: "What is the role of Mrs. Blorna, once known as 'Trude the Red,' and her husband, who sometimes describes himself as 'Leftist'? Dr. Blorna, highly paid corporation lawyer, with his wife Trude beside the swimming pool at their luxury home."

24

This is the moment for a kind of backing-up process, for what is known in movies and literature as a flashback: from the Saturday morning when Dr. and Mrs. Blorna, travel-worn and somewhat desperate, returned from their vacation, to the Friday morning when Katharina was once again taken to police headquarters for questioning, this time by Policewoman Pletzer and an older police officer who was only lightly armed, and she was picked up not from her own apartment but from Miss Woltersheim's, to which Katharina had driven around five o'clock that morning, this time in her car. The policewoman made no bones about knowing she would find Katharina at Miss Woltersheim's rather than at her own home. (In all justice we must not fail to recall the sacrifices and ordeals endured by Dr. and Mrs. Blorna: breaking off of their vacation, cab drive to the airport near I. Waiting in the fog. Cab to railway station. Catching the Frankfurt train plus changing at Munich. Being rattled about in the sleeper and, early in the morning, having hardly arrived home, already confronted by the *News*! Later—too late, of course—Blorna regretted that, instead of trying to telephone Katharina, who he knew was being questioned, he had not called Hach.)

What struck all those participating in Katharina's second interrogation on Friday—once again Moeding, Policewoman Pletzer, Public Prosecutors Korten and Hach, and Anna Lockster, stenographer (who was irritated by Blum's linguistic sensitivity and called her "stuck-up"—what struck all of these people was Beizmenne's mood of high good humor. He entered the room rubbing his hands, treated Katharina with great consideration, apologized for "certain incivilities" that stemmed from his own personality rather than his office, it was just that he was rather a rough diamond, and then started by picking up the itemized list that had been drawn up of all the confiscated articles. These were as follows:

1. One small, well-worn green notebook, containing nothing but telephone numbers; these had meanwhile been checked out and revealed nothing of a compromising nature. Katharina Blum had evidently been using this notebook for almost ten years. A handwriting expert who had been trying to trace Götten by his handwriting (Götten had been, among other things, an army deserter and had worked in an office, thus leaving a number of handwriting traces) had described the development of Katharina's handwriting as a classic example: the girl who at sixteen had made a note of the telephone number of Gerbers the butcher, at seventeen the number of Dr. Kluthen, physician, at twenty while working for Mr. Fehnern—and later—the numbers and addresses of caterers, restaurateurs, and those working in her own line of business.

2. Bank statements in which every transaction in her savings account had been meticulously identified by her own handwritten marginal notes. Each sum credited

or debited to the account—all correct and not one of them suspicious. The same applied to her entries and notes, contained in a small file, on the state of her commitments to the Haftex company, from which she had bought her apartment at "Elegant Riverside Residences." In addition her tax declarations, assessments, and payments had been thoroughly examined and checked out by an accountant, and nowhere could that expert discover any "substantial concealed amount." Beizmenne had considered it important to examine her financial transactions especially over the two preceding years, which he facetiously referred to as the "male visitor period." Nothing. However, it transpired that Katharina remitted 150 marks to her mother every month, and that she had a standing order with the firm of Kolter in Kuir for the care of her father's grave in Gemmelsbroich. The furniture she had bought, her household utensils, clothes, underwear, gasoline bills—all checked out and nowhere a discrepancy. In handing back the files to Beizmenne, the accountant remarked: "All I can say is, if she's released and is ever looking for a job— tip me off, will you? This is what we're always looking for and can never find." Nor did the Blum telephone bills yield any grounds for suspicion. It was apparent from them that she almost never made long-distance calls.

Further it was noted that now and again Katharina Blum had remitted small sums of 15 to 30 marks to her brother Kurt, then serving a sentence for breaking and entering, to augment his pocket money. Blum paid no church taxes. As shown by her financial records, she had left the Catholic Church at the age of nineteen in 1966.

3. A second small notebook with various entries, mainly figures, contained four columns: one for the Blorna household with amounts for grocery shopping and expenditures on cleaning materials, dry cleaning, laundry. From these entries it was clear that Katharina did all the ironing herself. The second column was for the Hiepertz home with similar details and accounts. A third was for her own home, which she evidently ran on a very modest bud-

get; there were months when she had spent scarcely 30 to 50 marks on food. However, she did seem to go quite often to the movies—she had no television set—and occasionally to buy herself chocolate bars and even a box of chocolates.

The fourth column itemized income and expenditure in connection with the extra jobs she took on and involved the purchase and laundering of uniforms as well as a proportion of the running expenses for her Volkswagen. At this point—the figures for gasoline—Beizmenne interrupted with an amiability that surprised everyone and asked her to account for the relatively high figures for gasoline, figures which, incidentally, tallied with the noticeably high figure on her odometer. It had been ascertained, he said, that the distance to the Blornas and back was about 6 kilometers, to the Hiepertzes and back about 8, to Miss Woltersheim's about 4, and if one were to reckon an average of one extra job a week (a generous estimate) and allow 20 kilometers for that (which was also generous and amounted to about 3 kilometers for each weekday) one would arrive at roughly 21 to 22 kilometers per day. And it must be considered that she did not visit Miss Woltersheim every day, but never mind about that. In other words, one arrived at some 8,000 kilometers a year, whereas when she—Katharina Blum—had acquired the VW six years ago the written agreement with Klormer the chef showed that at that time the car had had 56,000 kilometers on it. If one were to add six times 8,000 to that figure, her odometer should now show somewhere in the neighborhood of 104,000 to 105,000, whereas the actual figure was 162,000. Now it was known that from time to time she went to visit her mother in Gemmelsbroich and later at the sanatorium in Kuir-Hochsackel, and no doubt also her brother in jail— but the distance to Gemmelsbroich or Kuir-Hochsackel was about 50 kilometers there and back and to her brother about 60, and if one were to reckon one, or, to be generous, two visits a month (and her brother had been in jail only for the last year and a half, before that he had lived with their mother in Gemmelsbroich), well then—still calculating on the basis of six years—one would arrive at a further 7,000 to 8,000 kilometers, and there still remained a figure of between 45,000 and 50,000 unexplained, i.e., unaccounted for. So where had she driven to so often? Had she—he really didn't want to offer crude suggestions again, but she must understand his question—had she perhaps been meeting one or more persons somewhere—and, if so, where?

Fascinated, also shocked, not only Katharina Blum but all those present listened to Beizmenne's calculation presented in a mild voice, and it seemed as if Katharina, while Beizmenne was presenting these figures to her, did not even feel anger, merely a tension made up of shock and fascination, because, as he was speaking, she was not searching for an explanation of the 50,000 kilometers: she was trying to figure out where and when she had driven why and where to. On sitting down at the start of the interrogation she had been surprisingly approachable, almost "relaxed," she had even seemed a bit nervous and had accepted some tea without even insisting on paying for it herself. And now, when Beizmenne had finished with his questions and calculations, a deathly silence—to quote many, *almost* all, of those present—reigned, as if there were a feeling that someone, on the basis of a discovery which (had it not been for the gasoline bills) might easily have been overlooked, had now actually penetrated an intimate secret of Katharina Blum, whose life up to that moment had appeared to be an open book.

"Yes," said Katharina Blum, and from now on her statement was recorded and exists in the transcript, "that's right, that amounts to—I've just worked it out quickly in my head—almost 25 kilometers a day. I never gave a thought to it, nor to the cost either, but sometimes I would just drive off, simply get in the car and drive, with no destination in mind—or rather, somehow there always did turn out to be a destination, I mean I would drive in a

direction that just seemed to suggest itself, south toward
Coblenz, or west toward Aachen, or down to the Lower
Rhine. Not every day. I can't say how often or at what
intervals. Usually when it was raining and I had finished
work and was by myself. No, I wish to correct that statement: it was *only* when it was raining that I went for drives
like that. I don't know why exactly. You must remember
that sometimes, when I didn't have to go to the Hiepertzes
and had no extra job lined up, I would be home by five
o'clock with nothing to do. I didn't always want to go and
see Else, especially since she's become so friendly with
Konrad, and to go to the movies alone isn't always all that
safe for a woman on her own. Sometimes I would go and
sit in a church, not for religious reasons but because you
can be quiet there, but these days you find people button-
holing you in churches too, and they're not always laymen
either. I do have a few friends, of course: Werner Klormer,
for instance, from whom I bought my Volkswagen, and his
wife, and some of the other staff at Kloft's, but it is rather
difficult, and usually embarrassing, to turn up alone without automatically, or I should say, unconditionally, falling
in with every suggestion that offers. And so then I would
just get into the car, turn on the radio, and drive off, always on secondary roads, always in the rain, and the roads
I liked best were the ones with trees—sometimes I got as
far as Holland or Belgium, would have a cup of coffee or
a beer there, and drive home again. Yes. Now that you ask
me I see it all. So—if you ask me how often, I would say:
two or three times a month—sometimes less, sometimes
maybe more often, and usually for several hours, until at
about nine or ten, sometimes not till eleven, I would come
home, dead tired. It may have been partly fear too: I know
too many lonely women who spend their evenings getting
drunk in front of the TV."

The gentle smile with which Beizmenne absorbed this
explanation, without comment, gave no hint as to what
was going on in his mind. He merely nodded, and if he

rubbed his hands again it must have been because Katharina Blum's information had confirmed one of his theories. For a while everything was very quiet, as if those present were surprised or embarrassed; it seemed as if for the first time Blum had revealed something personal and intimate. After that the itemization of the remaining confiscated articles was swiftly disposed of.

4. One photograph album containing snapshots of persons who were all easily identified. Katharina Blum's father, who looked ailing and bitter and far older than he could have been. Her mother who, it was disclosed, was dying of cancer. Her brother. Katharina herself, at four, at six, as a First Communicant at ten, as a bride of twenty; her husband; the Gemmelsbroich pastor, neighbors, relatives, various photos of Else Woltersheim; then an older man, not immediately identifiable, who looked rather jolly and turned out to be Mr. Fehnern, the guilty accountant. Not a single picture of anyone who could be made to link up with Beizmenne's theories.

5. A passport issued in the name of Katharina Brettloh née Blum. In connection with this item, she was asked questions about travel, and it turned out that she had never "been on a real trip" and, except for a few days when she had been off sick, had always worked. She had received her vacation pay from the Fehnerns and the Blornas, but she had either gone on working or taken extra jobs.

6. One old chocolate box. Contents: some letters, scarcely a dozen, from her mother, brother, husband, Miss Woltersheim. None containing the slightest indication that bore on the suspicion resting upon her. The box also contained a few loose snapshots of her father as a private in the German Army and of her husband in the uniform of the Fife & Drum Corps, a few torn-off calendar pages with mottoes, and a sizable handwritten collection of her own recipes plus a pamphlet entitled "The Use of Sherry in Sauces."

7. One binder containing certificates, diplomas, and

records, all her divorce papers, and the certified documents relating to her condominium apartment.

8. Three bunches of keys. These had been checked out and found to be house and closet keys to her own apartment, the Blornas' home, and the Hiepertzes'.

It was established and recorded that no suspicious clue had been found among the above-mentioned articles; Katharina Blum's explanation of her gas consumption and the kilometers she had driven was accepted without comment.

Only now did Beizmenne draw from his pocket a ruby ring, set with diamonds, that he had apparently been keeping there loose, for he polished it on his jacket sleeve before holding it out to Katharina.

"Do you recognize this ring?"

"Yes," she said, without hesitation or embarrassment.

"Does it belong to you?"

"Yes."

"Do you know what it is worth?"

"Not exactly. It can't be much."

"Well now," said Beizmenne pleasantly, "we have had it appraised, and as a precautionary measure not only by our expert here in the building but also, so as to be sure and not do you an injustice, by a local jeweler. This ring is worth between eight and ten thousand marks. You didn't know that? I am prepared to believe you, but I must still ask you to explain where you got it. In the context of an inquiry concerning a criminal convicted of robbery and strongly suspected of murder, a ring of this kind is no trivial matter, nor is it a private and personal matter such as a few hundred kilometers or driving around for hours in the rain. Now from whom did you receive this ring? From Götten or the gentleman visitor, or perhaps Götten *was* the gentleman visitor? And if not: where did you drive to as a 'lady visitor,' if I may use the term facetiously—in the rain for thousands of kilometers? It would be a simple matter for us to find out from which jeweler the ring was obtained, and whether it was bought or stolen, but I would

like to give you a chance—I do not, you see, consider you
directly involved in a criminal capacity, merely naive and
a little too romantic. How do you propose to explain to
me—to us—that you, a person known to be easily shocked,
almost prudish, a person whose friends have nicknamed
'the nun,' who avoids discotheques because of the de-
praved goings-on there, who gets a divorce because her
husband 'made advances' to her—how do you propose to
explain that you (so you say) did not meet this man Götten
until the day before yesterday and yet that very day—one
might say, post haste—took him home and there very rap-
idly became, well, shall we say, intimate with him? What
do you call that? Love at first sight? Infatuation? Amorous
feelings? Don't you see that there are certain inconsisten-
cies there which do not altogether preclude suspicion? And
there is something else." He put his hand in his jacket
pocket and drew out a rather large white envelope from
which he extracted a somewhat fancy, mauve, cream-lined
envelope of normal dimensions. "This empty envelope
which, together with the ring, we found in your night-table
drawer, is postmarked February 12, 1974, 6:00 P.M., Düs-
seldorf Station Post Office—and addressed to you. For
Heaven's sake," Beizmenne said in conclusion, "if you
have had a boyfriend who visited you from time to time
and whom you sometimes drove to see, who wrote you
letters and sometimes gave you presents—go ahead and
tell us, it's not a crime! It would only incriminate you if
there were some connection with Götten."

It was clear to everyone in the room that Katharina
recognized the ring but had not known its value; that here
again the sensitive subject of male visitors was being
raised. Was she ashamed because she saw a threat to her
reputation, or did she see a threat to someone else whom
she did not want to implicate in the affair? This time she
only blushed slightly. Would she not admit to having received the ring from Götten because she knew it would
not have been very convincing to try and present Götten

as that kind of cavalier? She remained calm, "subdued" almost, as she testified:

"It is true that at Miss Woltersheim's party I danced exclusively and fervently with Ludwig Götten, whom I saw for the first time in my life and whose surname I did not discover until I was being questioned by the police on Thursday morning. I felt a great tenderness for him and he for me. I left Miss Woltersheim's apartment around ten o'clock and drove with Ludwig Götten to my apartment.

"As to the origin of the ring I cannot—correction: I do not wish to—give any information. Since it did not come into my possession in any irregular manner, I do not feel obliged to account for its origin. The sender of the envelope produced for my inspection is unknown to me. I take it to be one of the usual specimens of advertising material. I am by this time quite well known in the catering business. Why an advertisement should be sent to me with no sender's name in a fancy lined envelope is something I cannot explain. I would merely like to point out that some firms in the food business are anxious to project a glamorous image."

On then being asked why on that particular day, although she was obviously—and by her own admission—so fond of driving, why on that particular day she had taken the streetcar to Miss Woltersheim's, Katharina Blum said she had not known whether she would have a lot to drink or a little, and it had seemed safer not to take her own car. When asked whether she drank a lot or even sometimes became intoxicated, she said, No, she did not drink much and she had never been intoxicated, and only once—and that had been in the presence and at the instigation of her husband at a social evening of the Fife & Drum Corps—had she been *made* intoxicated, and that had been with some aniseed stuff that tasted like lemonade. Later she had been told that this somewhat expensive stuff was very popular for getting people drunk. When it was pointed out to her that this explanation—of having feared she might have too much to drink—did not hold water since she never drank much, and did she not realize that it must look as if she had had a regular assignation with Götten and so had known she would not need her car but would drive home in his, she shook her head, saying it was exactly as she had stated. She had certainly felt in the mood for drinking a bit more than usual, but in the end she had not done so.

One further point remained to be clarified before the lunch break: Why had she no savings book or checkbook? Maybe she did have a checking account somewhere after all? No, the only account she had was the one at the savings bank. Every sum at her disposal, even the smallest, she immediately applied to her loan, on which the interest was so high; sometimes this interest amounted to almost double the interest on her savings, and on a checking account there was hardly any interest at all. Besides, she found it too expensive and too complicated to use checks. All her running expenses, for her home and for her car, she paid in cash.

25

Certain blockages, also definable as tensions or pressures, are, of course, unavoidable inasmuch as not all sources can be diverted and/or rerouted at one go and all at once, so that dry land is immediately exposed. However, unnecessary tensions are to be avoided, and we will now try to explain why on this Friday morning not only Beizmenne but also Katharina behaved in such a mild, not to say subdued manner, Katharina seeming even nervous or intimidated. While it was true that the *News,* which a friendly neighbor had pushed under Miss Woltersheim's front door, had aroused anger, exasperation, indignation, shame, and fear in both women, the immediately ensuing telephone conversation with Blorna had mitigated these emotions; and since, shortly after the two horrified women

had skimmed through the *News* and Katharina had telephoned Blorna, Policewoman Pletzer had arrived and
frankly admitted that naturally Katharina's apartment was
being kept under surveillance and that was how she knew
she would find Katharina here, and now unfortunately
they had to go—Miss Woltersheim too, unfortunately—to
police headquarters for questioning, the shock caused by
the *News* gave way temporarily before Policewoman
Pletzer's candid, pleasant manner, and Katharina was once
again able to dwell on something that had occurred during
the night and that had made her very happy: Ludwig had
called her, and from *there*!

He had been so sweet, and that was why she had
told him nothing of all this trouble because she didn't
want him to feel he was the cause of any unhappiness.
Nor did they mention love, she had expressly forbidden
him to do that even on the way home with him in the car.
No, no, she was fine, of course she would rather be with
him and stay with him forever or at least for a long time,
preferably forever and ever, of course, and she would rest
up during Carnival and never, never again dance with
any other man but him, and never anything but Latin
American, and only with him, and what were things like
where he was? The accommodation was fine, and he
had everything he needed, and since she had forbidden
him to mention love all he wanted to say was that he
liked her very, very, very much, and one day—he didn't
yet know when, it might be months or even a couple
of years—he would come for her and take her away, he
didn't yet know where to. And so on, the way people do
chat on the phone when they feel a great affection for
one another. No mention of intimacies, let alone any
word about that event which Beizmenne (or, as becomes
increasingly likely: Hach) had so crudely specified. And
so on. Merely the things this kind of tender loving couple finds to say to each other. For quite some time. Ten
minutes. Maybe even more, Katharina told Else. Perhaps,
as far as the actual vocabulary of the two young lovers

is concerned, one may also refer to certain modern movies in which a good deal of chitchat plus a good deal of *seemingly* inconsequential chitchat goes on in telephone conversations—often over great distances.

The telephone conversation between Katharina and Ludwig had, moreover, been the cause of Beizmenne's relaxed and pleasant mood of leniency; and although he thought he knew why Katharina had dropped all that stubborn standoffish attitude, she, of course, could not suspect that his cheerful mood stemmed from the same event, although not for the same reason. (This notable and noteworthy process should prompt us to telephone more often—even, if need be, without tender whisperings—since we can never know *who* may derive pleasure from such a call.) But Beizmenne knew the reason for Katharina's nervousness, for he was also aware of a further telephone call, an anonymous one.

The reader is asked not to explore the sources of confidential information contained in this chapter: it is merely that the amateurishly erected earth wall of a subsidiary puddle has been breached and the water drawn off and/or caused to flow out before the weak retaining wall collapses and all that pressure and tension is drained away.

26

To avoid any misunderstanding it must be noted that naturally both Else Woltersheim and Blorna were aware that Katharina had committed an offense by helping Götten to slip out unseen from her apartment; indeed, the fact that she had provided him with an escape route made her an accessory to certain criminal acts, even if in this case not the relevant ones! Else Woltersheim told her this point-blank, shortly before Policewoman Pletzer came to pick them both up for questioning. Blorna seized the first opportunity to draw Katharina's attention to the criminal

nature of her action. Nor should Katharina's remark to
Miss Woltersheim about Götten be withheld: "But don't
you see—he was simply the One who was to come, and I
would have married him and had children with him—even
if I had had to wait years till he got out of jail!"

27

The interrogation of Katharina could thus be considered
at an end; she had merely to be available for a possible
confrontation with statements made by the other Woltersheim guests. For it was now necessary to clarify a question
that, in the context of Beizmenne's theory of a prearranged
assignation and conspiracy, was sufficiently important:
How had Ludwig Götten come to be a guest at the Woltersheim dance?

Katharina Blum was told that she could decide whether
to go home or to wait in some place of her choice, but she
declined to go home, saying that events had spoiled the
apartment for her once and for all, and that she preferred
to wait in a cell until Miss Woltersheim had been questioned, and then to go home with her. Only now did
Katharina take the two issues of the *News* from her handbag and ask whether the government—as she put it—
could not do something to protect her from this filth and
to restore her lost honor. She was now well aware that her
interrogation was perfectly justified, although she could
not quite see the point of this "going into every last intimate detail," but she could not understand how details
arising out of the interrogation—the gentlemen visitors,
for instance—could ever have come to the knowledge
of the *News,* and all those lying and fraudulent statements.
At this point Hach, the public prosecutor, intervened, saying that, in view of the enormous public interest in the
Götten case, it had, of course, been necessary to issue a
statement for the press; as yet there had been no press

conference, but owing to the excitement and apprehension generated by Götten's escape—which Katharina must remember she had made feasible—it would hardly be possible to avoid one. Moreover, the mere fact of knowing Götten had made her a "public figure" and thus the object of justifiable public interest. She was free to bring a private suit on the grounds of insulting and possibly libelous details in the newspaper reports and, if it should turn out that there had been "leaks" in official circles, she could rest assured that the police authorities would bring charges against a person or persons unknown and support her in the restitution of her rights.

Katharina Blum was then escorted to a cell. It was not considered necessary to put her under strict guard; she was assigned a fairly young woman police assistant, Renate Zündach, who stayed with her, unarmed, and reported later that throughout the whole period—some two and a half hours—Katharina Blum had done nothing but read the two issues of the *News* over and over again. Tea, sandwiches—she refused them all, not aggressively but in "quite a pleasant, rather apathetic way." Every attempt to discuss clothes, movies, dancing, which she, Renate Zündach, tried to initiate in order to take Blum's mind off her problems, had been repulsed by Katharina.

Then, Zündach reported, in order to help Blum, who seemed positively hypnotized by the *News,* she had asked her colleague Hüften to relieve her for a few minutes and had gone off to the archives, returning with clippings from other newspapers in which Blum's involvement and interrogation, and her potential role, had been reported quite matter-of-factly. They carried brief accounts on the third or fourth page that did not even give Blum's full name, referring merely to a certain Katharina B., a domestic. In the *Review,* for example, there had been a mere ten-line report, with no picture, in which mention was made of the unfortunate involvement of a completely blameless person. All this—she had placed fifteen newspaper clippings in front of Blum, she said—failed to con-

sole her: Katharina had merely asked: "Who reads those
anyway? Everyone *I* know reads the *News*!"

28

In order to clarify how Götten came to be at the Woltersheim dance, the first to be questioned was Else Woltersheim
herself, and from the outset it became clear that, in her
attitude toward the entire body of men by whom she was
being questioned, Miss Woltersheim was, if not downright hostile, certainly more hostile than Blum. She stated
that she had been born in 1930, was thus forty-four, un-
married, occupation housekeeper-cateress. Before testify-
ing about the affair itself she gave her opinion, in an
"unemotional, dry-as-dust tone of voice, which lent more
strength to her indignation than if she had shouted or
screamed abuse," on the treatment of Katharina Blum by
the *News* as well as on the fact that details from the interrogation were evidently being leaked to that kind of publication. She realized that Katharina's role had to be
examined, but she wondered if "the destruction of a
young life," as was now taking place, could be justified.
She had known Katharina, she went on, since the day she
was born, and could already observe the havoc being
wrought in her since yesterday. She was no psychologist,
but the fact that Katharina had obviously lost all interest
in her apartment, of which she had been so fond and for
which she had worked so hard, was, in her opinion,
alarming.

It was not easy to interrupt Miss Woltersheim's torrent
of complaint, it was too much even for Beizmenne, and
only when he broke in to reproach her for admitting
Götten into her home did she say that she hadn't even
known his name, he hadn't introduced himself nor had
anyone introduced him to her. All she knew was that, on

the Wednesday in question, at around 7:30 P.M., he had turned up in the company of Hertha Scheumel, who had come with her friend Claudia Sterm, who in turn was in the company of a man dressed as a sheikh of whom all she knew was that they called him Karl and who later in the evening behaved in a distinctly odd manner. There could be no question of any prearranged meeting with this man Götten, nor had she ever heard his name before, and she knew all about Katharina's life down to the last detail. On being confronted with Katharina's statement about her "mystery drives," she had perforce to admit that she had known nothing about them, and this dealt a crucial blow to her claim to familiarity with every detail of Katharina's life. On the subject of the gentlemen visitors she became embarrassed, saying that, since Katharina had apparently said nothing about them, she also would refuse to comment. The only thing she could say on this subject was: one of them had been a "rather corny affair," and "when I say corny I don't mean Katharina, I mean the visitor." If authorized by Katharina she would tell them all she knew about it; she thought it quite out of the question that Katharina's long drives had taken her to that person. Yes, this man did exist, and if she hesitated to say more about him it was because she did not want him to become a laughingstock. In any case, Katharina's part in both cases—that of Götten and of the gentleman visitor—had been quite beyond reproach. Katharina had always been a hardworking, respectable girl, a bit timid, or rather intimidated, and as a child she had even been a devout and faithful churchgoer. But then her mother, who used to clean the church in Gemmelsbroich, had been reprimanded several times for irregular behavior, and once she had even been caught sharing a bottle of sacramental wine with the verger in the sacristy. This had been blown up into an "orgy" and a scandal, and Katharina had had to suffer in school at the hands of the pastor. Yes, Mrs. Blum, Katharina's mother, had been very unstable and at times an alcoholic, but one must picture that husband—Katharina's father—always grumbling, always ailing, who had returned from the war a total wreck, then the embittered mother and the brother, who, one was bound to say, had turned out badly. She also knew the story of the marriage that had gone so hopelessly wrong. In fact, she had advised Katharina against it from the very beginning, Brettloh being an—she apologized for the expression—ass-licker, typical of those who kowtow to all authority, both secular and religious; besides, he was a most disgusting showoff. She had regarded Katharina's early marriage as a flight from her terrible home environment and, as was plain to see, the moment Katharina escaped from that environment and her imprudent marriage, she developed into a wonderful person. Her job qualifications were unimpeachable. That was something to which she—Miss Woltersheim—could attest not only verbally but also, if need be, in writing since she was a member of the Trade Council's examining board. With the growing trend in private and public entertaining toward what was now being called "organized buffet style," the opportunities for a woman like Katharina Blum were opening out accordingly, since she was a highly suitable person, as well as highly trained in organization, pricing, and attractive presentation. Although now, of course, if she failed to get satisfaction from the *News,* Katharina's interest in her career would fade along with her interest in her apartment.

At this point in her statement, Miss Woltersheim was informed that it was not the job of the police or the public prosecutor's office "to pursue certain undoubtedly reprehensible forms of journalism by bringing criminal charges." Freedom of the press was not to be lightly tampered with, and she could rest assured that a private complaint would be handled with justice and a charge on grounds of illegal sources of information brought against a person or persons unknown. It was Korten, the young public prosecutor, who, in an impassioned plea for freedom of the press and the right to protect the iden-

tity of sources of information, stressed that a person who
did not keep or fall into bad company could obviously
never give the press cause for wild and potentially damaging reporting.

The whole affair—that was to say, the sudden appearance of Götten and of the shadowy figure of Karl, the man
dressed as a sheikh—did, Korten must say, imply a strange
casualness in social intercourse. This had not as yet been
adequately explained to him, and he was counting on receiving plausible explanations during the interrogation of
the two young ladies concerned. She, Miss Woltersheim,
could not escape the reproach of having been less than
fastidious in the choice of her guests. Miss Woltersheim
refused to be taken to task in this way by a person consid-
erably younger than herself, and pointed out that she had
invited the two girls each to bring a friend, and that she
must say it was not her custom to ask her guests for their
friends' identification papers or a police certificate of good
conduct; whereupon she was rebuked and told that in this
instance age was not a factor whereas the status of the
public prosecutor, Mr. Korten, was, and a very considerable one at that. She must realize that the matter now
under investigation was a serious one, a grave, if not the
gravest, case of crime by violence, in which Götten, as
the evidence showed, was involved. She must leave it
to the state's legal representative to decide which details
and which admonishments were appropriate.

When asked once again whether Götten and the gentleman visitor could be one and the same person, Miss Woltersheim said No, there was absolutely no possibility of
that. But then when she was asked whether she knew the
"gentleman visitor" personally, whether she had ever seen
him or ever met him, she had to reply in the negative, and
since she had also been unaware of such an important
personal detail as the mysterious automobile drives her
testimony was termed unsatisfactory, and for the time
being she was dismissed "on a sour note." Before leaving
the room, obviously annoyed, she further declared that

Karl, the man dressed as a sheikh, had seemed to her at least as suspicious as Götten. In any event, he had kept talking to himself while in the washroom and had then disappeared without saying good-bye.

29

Since it was Hertha Scheumel, a salesgirl, aged seventeen, who had brought Götten to the party, she was the next to be interrogated. She was obviously nervous, saying she had never had anything to do with the police before, but then proceeded to offer a relatively plausible explanation for knowing Götten. "I live," she stated, "with my girl friend Claudia Sterm, who works in a chocolate factory, in a one-room apartment with kitchen and shower. We both come from Kuir-Oftersbroich and are both distantly related to Miss Woltersheim as well as to Katharina Blum" (although Miss Scheumel wished to describe the remoteness of the relationship in more detail by mentioning grandparents who had been cousins of grandparents, a precise degree of relationship was not deemed necessary and the term "distant" was regarded as adequate). "We call Miss Woltersheim Auntie and think of Katharina as a cousin.

"That evening, Wednesday, February 20, 1974, we were both, Claudia and I, in a real bind. We had promised Auntie Else to bring our boyfriends to her dance as otherwise there wouldn't be enough men to go around. Well, it so happened that my boyfriend, who is doing his military service in the Army at the moment, or, to be more exact, with the Engineers, has suddenly—as usual—been assigned to barracks duty, and although I suggested he simply take off I couldn't persuade him, because he'd already done that a few times and was scared of getting into real trouble. As for Claudia's boyfriend, by early afternoon he was so drunk we had to put him to bed. So we decided to go to the Café Polkt and pick up a couple of nice fellows there, since we didn't want to lose face with Auntie. There's always something going on at the café during Carnival time. People meet there before and after the dances and the Carnival ceremonies, and you can always be sure of finding lots of young people there.

"By late Wednesday afternoon the atmosphere at the café was already pretty good. I was twice asked to dance by this young man, and by the way I have only just learned that his name is Ludwig Götten and that he's a wanted criminal, and during the second dance I asked him if he wouldn't like to go to a party with me. He seemed delighted and agreed at once. He said he was just passing through, had no place to stay and no idea how he was going to spend the evening, and he would like to come with me very much. At the very moment when I was, you might say, fixing up a date with this Götten, Claudia happened to be dancing next to me with a man dressed as a sheikh, and I suppose they must have overheard what we were saying because the sheikh, who I learned later was called Karl, at once asked Claudia, in a kind of humble way which was meant to be funny, whether we couldn't find some small corner for him at this party as well, he was lonesome too and had no plans for the evening.

"Anyway, we'd got what we were after, and soon after that we drove in Ludwig's—I mean Mr. Götten's—car to Auntie Else's apartment. It was a Porsche, not very comfortable for four, but then we didn't have far to go. If I was asked whether Katharina Blum knew we were going to the Café Polkt to pick up a couple of fellows, I'd answer Yes. I had called her that morning at the Blornas, where she works, and told her that Claudia and I would have to go alone if we couldn't find anybody. I also told her we were going to the Café Polkt. She didn't think that was a good idea, she said we were too gullible, too irresponsible. But then we all know Katharina's funny about such things. That's why I was so surprised when Katharina grabbed hold of Götten almost immediately and danced with him the whole evening, as if they'd known each other all their lives."

30

Hertha Scheumel's statement was confirmed almost word for word by her friend Claudia Sterm. There was only one point, an insignificant one, in which they differed. She said she had danced three times, not twice, with the sheikh, because Karl had asked her to dance earlier than Götten had asked Hertha. And Claudia Sterm also expressed surprise at how quickly Katharina, who was always considered so standoffish, had become friendly, you might almost say familiar, with Götten.

31

There were three further guests at the party to be interrogated: Konrad Beiters, aged fifty-six, textile agent and friend of Miss Woltersheim's, and Mr. Georg Plotten (aged forty-two) and his wife Hedwig (aged thirty-six), both municipal employees. All three agreed in their account of the evening, from the arrival of Katharina Blum, of Hertha Scheumel accompanied by Ludwig Götten, and of Claudia Sterm accompanied by Karl in his sheikh costume. Furthermore, it had been a very nice evening, with dancing, and general conversation in which Karl had turned out to be especially amusing. The only wrong note—if you could call it that, for no doubt those two hadn't felt it to be one—was, according to Georg Plotten, the "total monopoly of Katharina Blum by Ludwig Götten." It had lent a serious, almost solemn note to the evening, something that wasn't too well suited to Carnival parties. Mrs. Hedwig Plotten stated that, after the departure of Katharina and Ludwig, when she had gone into the kitchen to get some more ice, she too had noticed Karl the sheikh talking to himself in the washroom. Moreover, this Karl had left shortly afterward, without saying good-bye.

32

Katharina Blum, brought back for questioning, confirmed her telephone conversation with Hertha Scheumel but persisted in her denial that it had concerned any arrangement for a meeting with Götten, for it was suggested to her—not by Beizmenne but by Korten, the younger of the two prosecutors—that she would do well to admit that Götten had called her up after her telephone conversation with Hertha Scheumel, and that she had been smart enough to send Götten to the Café Polkt and have him get into conversation with Hertha Scheumel so that he could meet her (Katharina) at Miss Woltersheim's without attracting attention. This had been easy enough to do since Miss Scheumel was a striking blonde, somewhat flashily dressed. Katharina Blum, by now almost totally apathetic, merely shook her head as she sat there still clutching the two issues of the *News*. She was then dismissed and, together with Miss Woltersheim and Konrad Beiters, left police headquarters.

33

In discussing the signed depositions and rechecking them for possible gaps, Korten raised the question of whether some serious effort should not be made to bring in this

sheikh by the name of Karl and investigate his highly ob-
scure role in the affair. He must say he was very surprised
that no measures had been taken to trace this "Karl."
After all, this Karl had obviously turned up simultane-
ously, if not together, with Götten at the Café Polkt and
had likewise "crashed" the party, and to him—Korten—
his role appeared mysterious if not suspicious.

At this point all those present burst out laughing; even
the normally reserved Policewoman Pletzer permitted
herself a smile. The stenographer, Mrs. Anna Lockster,
laughed so raucously that she had to be called to order by
Beizmenne. And finally, since Korten still had not understood, his colleague Hach enlightened him. Had Korten
not realized, or noticed, that Commissioner Beizmenne
had deliberately passed over or failed to mention the
sheikh? Surely it was obvious that he was "one of our
men" and that the alleged monologue in the washroom
was nothing more than a method—clumsily executed,
it was true—of instructing his colleagues by pocket trans-
mitter to start shadowing Götten and Blum, for of course
by this time Blum's address was known. "And no doubt
you also realize, Mr. Korten, that during Carnival time
sheikh costumes are the ideal disguise, since nowadays,
for obvious reasons, sheikhs are more popular than cowboys." And Beizmenne added: "Of course, we realized
right away that the Carnival would make it easier for the
lawbreakers to drop out of sight and more difficult for us
to remain hot on the trail, Götten having been tailed for
the past thirty-six hours. Götten—who, by the way, was
not disguised—had spent the night in a VW bus on the
parking lot from which he later stole the Porsche, and he
had breakfast in a café where he then shaved and
changed in the washroom. We didn't lose sight of him for
a single minute, we had about a dozen policemen disguised as sheikhs, cowboys, and Spaniards on his tail, all
equipped with pocket transmitters and acting like revelers
somewhat the worse for wear, ready to report instantly on

any attempts at contact. The persons Götten contacted before entering the Café Polkt have all been traced and checked out:

a bartender at whose counter he had a beer;

two girls with whom he danced at a nightclub in the old quarter of the town;

a gas-station attendant near the Holzmarkt who filled up the stolen Porsche;

a man at the newsstand on Matthias-Strasse;

a sales clerk (male) in a tobacco store;

a bank teller at whose window he changed seven hundred U.S. dollars which probably originated from a bank holdup.

"All these persons have been identified unequivocally as chance encounters rather than planned contacts, and none of the words exchanged with each individual person suggests a code. However, I will not be persuaded that Miss Blum was also a chance encounter. Her telephone conversation with Miss Scheumel, the punctuality with which she turned up at Miss Woltersheim's, and that damned intimacy with which the two of them danced right from the very first second—and the speed with which they made off together—everything speaks against chance. But, above all, the fact that she apparently let him leave without saying good-bye and quite obviously showed him a way out of the apartment building that must have been overlooked by our strict surveillance. The apartment building—that is, the building within the apartment complex where she lives—was never out of our sight for one moment. Of course, we could not keep the entire area of almost one and a half square kilometers under complete surveillance. She must have known an escape route and shown it to him; besides, I am certain that she found a hideout for him—and possibly others too—and knows exactly where he is. The buildings of her employers have already been checked out, we have made inquiries in her own village, and Miss Woltersheim's apartment has again been thoroughly searched while she was here for questioning. Nothing. In my opinion the best thing would be to let her run around freely so she can make a mistake, and probably the trail will lead to his present quarters via that mysterious gentleman visitor, and I am certain that the trail to the escape route inside the apartment building leads via Mrs. Blorna, whom we now know also as 'Trude the Red' and who was one of the architects who designed the apartment complex."

34

This brings us to the end of the first backing-up process, we have moved from the Friday to the Saturday. Everything will be done to avoid further blockages and unnecessary buildups of tension. It will probably not be possible to avoid them entirely.

However, it may be illuminating to note that, after the final interrogation on Friday afternoon, Katharina Blum asked Else Woltersheim and Konrad Beiters to drive her first to her apartment and—please, please—to go up with her. She told them she was scared: during that Thursday night, shortly after her telephone conversation with Götten (any outsider should recognize her innocence from the fact that she spoke openly, although not while being questioned, about her telephone contacts with Götten!) something absolutely revolting had happened. Almost immediately after her call from Götten, in fact she had hardly replaced the receiver, the phone rang again, and in the "wild hope" that it was Götten again she had at once picked up the receiver, but instead of Götten on the line it had been a "horribly soft" male voice "whispering" a whole string of "nasty things" to her, wicked things, and the worst of it was that the fellow had said he lived in the same building and why, if she was so keen on intimacies, did she look for them so far away, he was willing and able to offer her every conceivable variety of intimacy. Yes, it was because of this phone call that she had gone to Else's that same night. She was scared, scared of the phone even, and, since Götten had her phone number although she didn't have Götten's, she was still hoping for a call while at the same time being scared of the phone.

Well, we must not withhold the fact that there were more scares in store for Katharina Blum. To begin with: her mailbox, which so far had played a very insignificant role in her life and which she generally glanced into simply "because everyone does" but without success. On this Friday morning it was full to overflowing, and in a manner far from delighting Katharina. For, although Else W. and Beiters did their utmost to intercept her mail, she would not be deterred and, presumably in the hope of some sign of life from her dear Ludwig, looked through all the letters and circulars—totaling about twenty— evidently without finding anything from Ludwig, and stuffed the whole bundle into her handbag. Even the ride up in the elevator was an ordeal since two other occupants of the building were riding up too. One man (it must be said, improbable though it may sound) dressed as a sheikh, who squeezed himself into a corner in an agony of attempted dissociation but fortunately got out at the fourth floor; and a woman (what's true is true, crazy though it may sound) dressed as an Andalusian, and this person, protected by her mask, far from moving away from Katharina remained standing directly beside her, looking her up and down with brazen curiosity out of "impudent, hard brown eyes." She continued up beyond the eighth floor.

Warning: there is worse to come. When she had finally reached her apartment, clinging to Beiters and Miss W. as she walked in, the telephone rang, and here Miss W. was quicker than Katharina: shaking off Katharina she ran to pick up the receiver, they saw her horrified expression, saw her turn pale, heard her "You filthy bitch, you filthy cowardly bitch," and instead of replacing the receiver she craftily put it down beside the cradle.

In vain did Miss W. and Beiters try to part Katharina from her mail: she kept the bundle of letters and circulars firmly clutched in her hands, together with the two issues of the *News* that she had also taken from her bag, and insisted on opening it all. It was useless. She read every one!

Not all of it was anonymous. One letter that was not anonymous—the most detailed—came from a firm calling itself "Mail Orders Intimate" and offering her every variety of sex article. For a person of Katharina's sensibility, this was pretty strong stuff, and even worse was that someone had written by hand in the margin: "*These* are the genuine articles!" In short—or, better still, in statistical terms—the other eighteen items of mail were:

seven anonymous postcards, handwritten with "crude" sexual propositions that in one way or another all included the words "Communist bitch";

four more anonymous postcards containing insulting political remarks but no sexual propositions. These remarks ranged from "Red agitator" to "Kremlin stooge";

five letters containing clippings from the *News*, most of which (some three or four) had comments written in red ink in the margins such as: "Where Stalin failed, you'll fail too";

two letters containing religious exhortations, and on the tracts enclosed with them was written: "You must learn to pray again, you poor lost child," and "Kneel down and confess, God has not yet abandoned you."

And only now did Else W. discover a piece of paper that had been pushed under the door and which fortunately she was able to hide from Katharina: "Why don't you make use of my sex catalogue? Do I have to force your happiness on you? Your neighbor, whom you have so haughtily rejected. I am warning you." This had been printed in script from which Else W. thought she could deduce a college education if not medical training.

35

It is, surely, astonishing that neither Miss W. nor Konrad B. was astonished when, with no thought of intervening in any way, they watched Katharina walk to the little bar in her living room, take out one bottle each of sherry, whiskey, and red wine and a half-empty bottle of cherry syrup and, with no visible sign of emotion, throw them against the immaculate walls, where they smashed and spewed their contents.

She did the same in her little kitchen, using tomato ketchup, salad dressing, vinegar, and Worcester sauce for the same purpose. Must we add that she did the same in her bathroom with tubes and jars of face cream, powder, and bath oil—and in her bedroom with a bottle of eau de cologne?

Through it all she appeared so systematic, so impassive, so convinced and convincing, that Else W. and Konrad B. never lifted a finger.

36

Naturally there have been a good many theories aimed at pinpointing the exact moment in time at which Katharina first formed her intention to commit a murder or devised her plan for murder and decided to carry it out. Some people think that first article in Thursday's *News* did the trick; others regard Friday as the crucial day because that day the *News* was still stirring up trouble and destroying (subjectively, at least) her neighborhood and the apartment of which she was so fond; then came the anonymous caller, the anonymous mail—and to cap it all the *News* of Saturday, plus (here we are looking ahead!) the *Sunday News*. Surely such speculations are idle: she planned the murder and carried it out—and that's that! Without a doubt something in her "came to a head"—the statements of her former husband particularly upset her, and we can be certain that the contents of the *Sunday News,* if not actually the trigger, must have had a far from soothing effect on her.

37

Before our flashback may be regarded as complete and we can focus once again on Saturday, it remains necessary to describe Friday evening and Friday night at Miss Woltersheim's. Overall conclusion: surprisingly peaceful. True, attempts by Konrad Beiters to distract Katharina by putting on some dance records, even Latin American ones, and asking her to dance were not a success, nor was the attempt to part Katharina from the *News* and her anonymous mail; attempts to make out that the whole thing wasn't all that important and would soon pass also came to nothing. She'd been through worse, hadn't she? Her miserable childhood, her marriage with that wretch Brettloh, the alcoholism and, "to put it mildly, the depravity of your mother who, when all's said and done, is responsible for Kurt's leaving the straight and narrow." Wasn't Götten safe, at least for the time being, and his promise to come for her to be taken seriously? Wasn't it Carnival, and wasn't her financial position secure? Weren't there all those nice people like the Blornas and the Hiepertzes, and wasn't even that "conceited jackass"—there was still some reluctance to name the gentleman visitor by name—actually quite an amusing character and far from sinister?

Katharina would have none of this and reminded them of the "stupid ring and that silly fancy envelope" that had got them both into such a terrible jam and might even have brought suspicion on Ludwig. Could she ever have known that that jackass would spend all that money for the sake of his vanity? No indeed, she certainly couldn't call him amusing. No.

When they turned to practical matters—whether, for instance, she should look for a new apartment and whether it wasn't time to discuss where—Katharina became evasive, saying the only practical matter she had in mind was to make herself a Carnival costume, and she asked Else to lend her a big sheet since, in view of the vogue for sheikhs, she intended to "join the crowds" on Saturday or Sunday dressed as a Bedouin woman. So what's happened that is so bad? Scarcely a thing, if you look at it closely or, to be more precise: almost everything has been good, for isn't it a fact that Katharina has met "the One who was to come," hasn't she "spent a night of romance" with him? Granted, she has been questioned, or rather interrogated, and it is clear that Ludwig is no mere "butterfly hunter." Then there has been the usual filth in the *News,* a few filthy beasts have made anonymous phone calls, others have written anonymous letters. But doesn't life go on? Isn't Ludwig being well—in fact comfortably—provided for, as she and only she knows? Now we're fixing up a Carnival costume which will make Katharina look delightful, a white burnous; how pretty she'll look when she "joins the crowds" in it!

Finally even Nature demands her due, and one falls asleep, dozes off, wakes up again, dozes off again. How about a little drink? Why not? Peace and quiet reign: a young woman fallen asleep over her sewing while an older man and woman move cautiously around her "so as not to interfere with Nature." Nature is so little interfered with that Katharina is not even roused by the telephone when it rings around two-thirty in the morning. Why do the hands of sober Else Woltersheim start trembling as she lifts the receiver? Is she expecting anonymous intimacies such as she heard a few hours ago? Mind you, two-thirty in the morning is an alarming hour for anyone to call, but she grabs the receiver, which Beiters snatches from her, and when he says "Yes?" the receiver at the other end is replaced immediately. And it rings again, and again—the moment he picks it up, even before he says "Yes?"—the caller replaces the receiver. Naturally there are people who want to turn a person into a nervous wreck once they've got one's name and address from the *News*, and the best thing is not to replace the receiver.

And at that point it is decided to shield Katharina at least from the Saturday edition of the *News*; but Katharina has taken advantage of a few moments while Else W. is asleep and Konrad B. is shaving in the bathroom, and she has crept out onto the street, where in the early-morning light she has flung open the first *News*box she comes to and committed a kind of sacrilege: she has abused the CONFIDENCE of the *News* by taking a *News*paper without paying for it! At this juncture our flashback may be considered temporarily complete, this being the very hour at which the Blornas, this same Saturday, travel-worn, irritable, and depressed, leave the night train and pick up that same edition of the *News*, to be studied when they get home.

38

At the Blorna home it is a depressing Saturday morning, extremely depressing in fact, not only because of an almost sleepless night of being rattled and jolted about in the sleeper, not only because of the *News*, which, to quote

Mrs. Blorna, pursues one like the plague wherever one goes, one isn't safe anywhere; depressing not only because of the reproachful telegrams sent by influential friends, business acquaintances, and "Lüstra" (LÜding & STRÄubleder Investments) but also because of Hach, whom they call too early in the day, too early, that's all (and yet too late when they reflect that they would have done better to call him on Thursday). He could hardly be described as cordial, told them that Katharina's interrogation was over, couldn't say whether proceedings would be taken against her, at the moment she certainly needed support but so far not legal support. Had they forgotten it was Carnival and that even public prosecutors had the right to some free time and a bit of celebrating? Well, of course, they had known each other for twenty-four years, had been at university together, crammed together, sung together, even hiked together, and one is not going to let a few minutes of grumpiness upset one, especially since one is feeling so extremely depressed oneself, but then came the request—and from a public prosecutor!—to continue the discussion in person rather than over the long-distance phone. Yes, there was a certain amount of incriminating evidence against her, there was much that needed explaining, but no more now, maybe later that afternoon, when they could be together. Where? In town. They would walk up and down somewhere, that would be best. In the lobby of the museum. At four-thirty. No phone calls to Katharina's apartment, none to Miss Woltersheim, none to Mr. and Mrs. Hiepertz.

It was also depressing to find that the absence of Katharina's orderly hand made itself felt with such speed and clarity. How in the world did it happen that within half an hour—though all they had done was to make some coffee, get out some rye crisp, butter, and honey, and place their few pieces of baggage in the hall—chaos seemed already to have broken loose, and finally even Trude became irritable because he kept on asking her how she could possibly see any connection between Katharina's affair and Alois Sträubleder, let alone Lüding, and she didn't do a thing to help him, merely pointing, in her mock naive-ironic way, which at other times he liked but did not appreciate at all this morning, to the two issues of the *News,* and hadn't he been struck by one phrase in particular, and when he asked her what phrase she refused to tell him, remarking sarcastically that she wanted to test his perspicuity, and he read "this filth, this damn filth, that pursues a person wherever he goes," over and over again, not concentrating because the anger over his twisted statement and "Trude the Red" kept mounting in him afresh, until he finally capitulated and humbly asked Trude to help him out; he was so beside himself, he said, that his perspicuity failed him; besides, for years he had been only a corporation lawyer, had done scarcely any criminal work at all, to which she replied dryly, "Too bad," but then showed some mercy by saying, "You mean you didn't notice the phrase 'gentleman visitor,' or that I connected that phrase with the telegrams? Would anyone ever describe this Götting—no, Götten—just have a good look at his pictures again, would anyone ever describe him, no matter how he was dressed, as a 'gentleman visitor'? No, you must agree that someone like that would only be called a 'male visitor' in the language of amateur informers living in the building, and I'll turn myself into a prophet here and now and tell you that within one hour at the most we shall also be receiving a gentleman visitor, and another thing I'll prophesy is: trouble, confrontation—and possibly the end of an old friendship, trouble too with your Trude the Red and more than trouble with Katharina, who has two fatal characteristics: loyalty and pride, and she will never, never admit that she showed this boy an escape route, one which we—she and I—had looked over together. Take it easy, dear heart, take it easy: it'll never come out, but to tell the truth I'm the one responsible for this Götting, no Götten, vanishing from her apartment without being seen. I don't suppose you remember, but I had a diagram of the entire heating, ventilation, plumbing, and cable systems of 'Elegant Riverside Residences' hanging in my bedroom. It showed the heating ducts in red, the ventilation ducts in blue, the cables in green, and the plumbing in yellow. This diagram fascinated Katharina to such a degree—and you know what a person she is for order and planning, in fact she's positively brilliant at it—that she would stand in front of it for a long time and keep asking me about the relationships and significance of this 'abstract painting' as she called it, and I was just about to get hold of a copy and give it to her. I'm rather relieved I didn't, imagine if they'd found a copy of the diagram in her apartment—that would have been the best kind of support for the conspiracy theory, the idea of an arms depot, the link between 'Trude-the-Red-and-outlaws' and 'Katharina-and-gentleman-visitor.' Naturally a diagram like that would be an ideal guide for all kinds of intruders—burglars, lovers, whatever—who wanted to come and go without being seen. I even explained the height of the various passages to her: where you can walk upright, where you have to duck, where you have to crawl, when pipes burst or cables break down. This is the only possible way our fine young gentleman, whose caresses she can now only dream about, can have slipped through the police, and if he's really a bank robber he'll have tumbled to the system at once. Maybe that's how the gentleman visitor went in and out too. These modern apartment blocks require totally different methods of surveillance from the old-fashioned apartment buildings. Sometime or other you must tip off the police and the public prosecutor's office. They watch the main entrances, and possibly the lobby and elevator, but there's also a service elevator leading directly to the basement—and there a person can crawl a few hundred yards, lift up a manhole cover somewhere, and vanish into thin air. Believe me, there's nothing to do now but pray, for the last thing Alois needs is *News* headlines in any shape or form. What he needs now is for the findings

and the reports on them to be thoroughly doctored, and
what he's just as scared of as headlines is the sourpuss
expression of one Maud, his well and truly wedded wife,
by whom, incidentally, he has four children. You mean
to say you've never noticed how 'boyishly gay,' how
'high-spirited,' he was—and, I must say, he couldn't have
been nicer the few times he danced with Katharina, and
how he positively insisted on driving her home—and how
boyishly disappointed he was when she got her own car?
The very thing he needed, the very thing his heart desired—an exceptionally nice young person like Katharina,
not 'fast' and yet—what do you men call it?—with a
capacity for love, serious and yet young, and prettier than
she ever realized. Hasn't she sometimes gladdened your
manly heart a bit?"

Yes, of course she had: gladdened his manly heart, and
he admitted it, and also admitted that he did more, much
more, than just like her, and she, Trude, must know that
everyone, not only men, sometimes had strange impulses
just to take someone in their arms, and maybe more—
but Katharina, no, there was something about her that
could never, never have made him one of her gentlemen
visitors, and if something had held him back, indeed made
it impossible for him to become—or should he say, try to
become—one it wasn't, and she knew how he meant this, it
wasn't respect for her, Trude, or consideration for her, but
respect for Katharina—that was it, respect, you might say
reverence, more, *fond* reverence for her, hell, innocence—
and more, more than innocence, something he couldn't find
the right word for. It must be that strange, warmhearted
reserve of Katharina's and—although he was fifteen years
her senior and God knew he had done pretty well in life—
the way Katharina had set to work to plan and organize
her ruined life—it was this that had held him back, if he
had ever had any such ideas, because he had been afraid of
destroying her or her life—she was so vulnerable, so damn
vulnerable, and if it turned out that Alois actually had been

her gentleman visitor he would—to put it plainly—"punch him in the jaw"; yes, they must help, help her, those tricks and interrogations and questionings were more than she could handle—and now it was too late, and somehow or other he must find Katharina before the day was out . . . but at this point he was interrupted in his revelatory musings by Trude remarking, in her inimitable wry manner: "The gentleman visitor has just driven up."

39

It must be established here and now that Blorna did not punch Sträubleder in the jaw, although indeed it was he driving up in a flashy rented car. It is our wish not only that as little blood should flow here as possible, but also that the portrayal of physical violence, if it must be mentioned at all, should be kept to the minimum required by our reportorial obligations. This does not mean that the atmosphere at the Blornas became less depressing; on the contrary, it became more depressing than ever, for Trude B. could not resist greeting their old friend, as she went on stirring her coffee, with the words: "Hullo there, gentleman visitor." "I assume," said Blorna in embarrassment, "that Trude has once again hit the nail on the head." "Yes," said Sträubleder, "I just wonder whether that's always so tactful."

Here it may be noted that the relationship between Mrs. Blorna and Alois Sträubleder had once become almost unbearably strained when he had tried, if not exactly to seduce her, certainly to make a pass at her and she in her dry way had given him to understand that, irresistible though he might be in his own eyes, he was not so in hers. In these circumstances it will be understood why Blorna escorted Sträubleder immediately to his study and asked his wife to leave them alone together and in the interval

("interval between what?" asked Mrs. Blorna) to make
every possible effort to locate Katharina.

40

Why does one suddenly find one's own study so repulsive,
everything upside down and dirty although there is not a
speck of dust to be seen and everything is in its proper
place? What makes the red leather armchairs, in which
one has clinched many a good business deal and had many
a confidential chat, in which one can be really relaxed
and listen to music, suddenly seem so repulsive, even the
bookshelves disgusting and the signed Chagall on the wall
downright suspect, as if it were a fake done by the art-
ist himself? Ashtrays, lighters, whiskey decanter—what
makes one dislike these harmless if expensive objects?
What makes such a depressing day after an extremely depressing night so intolerable and the tension between old
friends so powerful that sparks are ready to fly? Why does
one dislike the walls, stippled in soft yellow and adorned
with contemporary graphic art?

"It's like this," said Alois Sträubleder, "I really only
came to tell you that I no longer need your help in *this*
affair. You lost your nerve again, out there at the airport
in the fog. An hour after you both lost your nerve or your
patience the fog lifted, and you could still have been here
by 6:30 in the evening. If you'd thought it over quietly,
you could have called the airport in Munich and found
out that flights were leaving on time again. But never
mind about that. To be perfectly honest with you—even
if there'd been no fog and the plane *had* left on time,
you'd have got here too late because the crucial part of
the questioning was over long before and there'd have
been nothing left for you to prevent."

"I'm no match for the *News* anyway," said Blorna.

"The *News*," said Sträubleder, "is no threat, Lüding's seen to that, but there are other papers, and I don't mind any kind of headline except this kind that associates me with outlaws. If an affair with a woman gets me into trouble, it's private trouble, not public. Even a picture of me with a woman as attractive as Katharina Blum wouldn't harm me, and by the way they're dropping the theory of the male visitor, and neither the ring nor the letter—well yes, I did give her a rather valuable ring, which they've found, and I did write her a few letters, of which all they've found is one envelope—neither of those things is going to present a problem. The bad part is that this Tötges uses a different name when he writes things for the weeklies which the *News* is not allowed to print, and that—well— Katharina has promised him an exclusive interview. I just found this out a few minutes ago, from Lüding, what's more he's glad Tötges is taking up the offer since, as I say, the *News* has been taken care of, but we've no influence on Tötges's other journalistic activities, he handles those through a go-between. You don't seem to be in the picture at all, do you?"

"I've no idea what's going on," said Blorna.

"An odd state of affairs for an attorney whose client I am, I must say; that comes from frittering away one's time in rattling trains instead of getting in touch with weather bureaus which could have told one that the fog would soon lift. So you haven't been in touch with her yet?"

"No, have you?"

"No, not directly. I only know that about an hour ago she called the *News* and promised Tötges an exclusive interview for tomorrow afternoon. He accepted. And there's something else that worries me more, much much more, it's tying my stomach in knots" (here Sträubleder's face showed something like emotion and his voice became strained), "starting tomorrow you can say what you like about me, and as much as you like, because it's true that I've abused your confidence and Trude's—but on the other hand we do live in a free country where it's permitted to lead a free love life, and you must believe me when I say I would do anything to help her, I would even gamble my reputation, for—go ahead, laugh—I love that woman, but: she's beyond helping—*I* can still use some help—she simply won't let herself be helped. . . ."

"And is there no way you can help her, protect her from the *News,* from those bastards?"

"Now listen, you mustn't take that business with the *News* so seriously, even if they have rather got their claws into you and Trude. For God's sake let's not quarrel now over the yellow press and the freedom of the press. I'll come to the point: I'd appreciate it if you could be present at the interview as my attorney *and* hers. You see, the really devastating part still hasn't come out either in the interrogations or in the press: six months ago I induced her to accept a key to our country place in Kohlforstenheim. They didn't find the key when they searched either the house or Katharina, but she *has* it, or at least she did have it, if she hasn't just thrown it away. It was just a sentimental impulse on my part, call it what you like, but I wanted her to have a key to the house because I refused to give up hope that she would come to me there one day. You must believe that I would help her, that I'd stand by her, that I'd even go to them and confess: Look, *I*'m the mysterious visitor—but I know only too well: while she'd let me down, she'd never let down that Ludwig of hers."

There was something quite new, unexpected, in Sträubleder's expression, something that aroused, if not pity, at least curiosity in Blorna; it was a kind of humility, or was it jealousy?

"What's all this about jewelry and letters and now a key?"

"For God's sake, Hubert, don't you get it yet? It's something I can't tell either Lüding or Hach or the police—I'm convinced she's given the key to that fellow Ludwig and that that's where he's been hiding out the past two days. I'm scared, I tell you, about Katharina, about the police, and about that young idiot too who may be hiding out in my house in Kohlforstenheim. I'd like him to disappear before they find him, but at the same time I'd like them to catch him, to put an end to the whole business. Now do you get it? What's your advice?"

"You might call up there, in Kohlforstenheim, it seems to me."

"And do you really believe that if he's there he'll answer the phone?"

"All right, then you must call the police, there's no alternative. If only to prevent a disaster. Call them anonymously, if you must. If there's even the slightest possibility that Götten is at your place out there, you must notify the police immediately. Otherwise I will."

"So that my house and name get linked up in the headlines with that outlaw after all? I had a different idea. . . . I was thinking maybe you could drive out there, I mean to Kohlforstenheim, as my attorney, sort of, just to make sure the place is all right."

"At this moment in time? On Carnival Saturday, with the *News* already aware that I've abruptly broken off my vacation—and I'm supposed to have done that just to make sure everything's all right at your place in the country? The fridge still working, hm? The thermostat still set properly, no windows smashed, enough liquor in the bar and the sheets not damp? And for that an eminent corporation lawyer, owner of a luxury villa with a swimming pool and married to 'Trude the Red,' comes rushing back from his vacation? Do you really think that's such a smart idea, when we may be certain that the gentlemen from the *News* are watching my every move—and there I go driving, straight from the sleeper as it were, out to your country home to see if the crocuses will soon be peeking through or the snowdrops are already out? Do you really think that's such a great idea—quite apart from the fact that our friend Ludwig has already proved he's a pretty good shot?"

"Hell, I'm not sure whether your wisecracks are so

appropriate right now. I ask you, as my attorney and my friend, to render me a service, and not even an especially personal one at that, really more a kind of citizen's duty—and you come back at me with snowdrops. Since yesterday this affair's been kept so secret that we haven't had so much as a grain of information out of them since this morning. All we know is what we read in the *News,* and we're lucky that Lüding has enough pull there. The public prosecutor's office and the police have even stopped calling the Ministry of the Interior, and Lüding has pull there too. It's a matter of life and death, Hubert."

Just then Trude entered without knocking, carrying the transistor radio and saying quietly: "No longer of death, only of life, thank God. They've caught the boy, he was stupid enough to shoot and so they shot at him, he's wounded but in no danger. In your garden, Alois, out in Kohlforstenheim, between the swimming pool and the pergola. They describe it as the super-luxury villa of one of Lüding's cronies. Incidentally, there's still such a thing as a true gentleman: the first thing our friend Ludwig said was that Katharina had absolutely nothing to do with the whole business, it was a purely private love affair totally unrelated to the crimes with which he was charged but which he continued to deny. You'll probably have to have a few windows replaced, Alois—they banged around there quite a bit. Your name hasn't cropped up yet, but maybe you should call Maud, she must be upset and in need of consolation. By the way, they caught three of Götten's alleged accomplices at the same time, in other places. The whole thing is called a triumph for a certain Commissioner Beizmenne. And now get going, Alois my dear, and this time call on your wife for a change—maybe she could do with a gentleman visitor."

It is not hard to imagine that at this point Blorna's study came close to being the scene of a physical confrontation definitely not in keeping with the surroundings and furnishings of the room. Sträubleder allegedly—*allegedly*—flew at Trude's throat but was prevented by her husband, who pointed out to him that surely he did not intend to attack a lady. Sträubleder allegedly—*allegedly*—said that he wasn't sure whether the term "lady" applied to such a shrew, and there were some words that in certain circumstances, and especially in the wake of tragic events, should not be used sarcastically, and those words were loaded, and if he heard them once more, just once more, then— yes, what then—well, that would be the end. He had scarcely left the house and Blorna had had no chance to tell Trude that maybe she *had* gone a bit far when she cut in with: "Katharina's mother died last night. I did manage to locate her: she's in Kuir-Hochsackel."

41

Before embarking on our final diversion and rerouting maneuvers we must be permitted to make the following "technical" interjection. Too much is happening in this story. To an embarrassing, almost ungovernable degree, it is pregnant with action: to its disadvantage. Naturally it is to be deplored when a self-employed housekeeper shoots and kills a reporter, and a case of this kind undoubtedly has to be cleared up or at least an attempt must be made to do so. But what is to be done with successful attorneys who break off their hard-earned skiing vacations for the sake of a housekeeper? With industrialists (who are professors and politicos on the side) who in their callow sentimental way simply force keys to country homes (and themselves) on this housekeeper, in both cases unavailingly, as we know, and who want publicity, but only of a certain kind; with a whole raft of objects and people whom it is impossible to synchronize and who continually disturb the flow (i.e., the linear course of events), because they are, shall we say, immune? What is to be done with crime commissioners who continually, and successfully, demand "little plugs"? In a nutshell: it is all too full of

holes, and yet, at what is for the narrator the crucial moment, not full enough, because, while it is possible to learn
of this or that (from Hach, maybe, and a few male and female police officials), nothing, absolutely nothing of what
they say holds water because it would never be confirmed
by or even stated in a court of law. It is not conclusive
evidence! It has not the slightest public value.

For example, this whole business of "little plugs." Of
course, wiretapping yields information, but that very information—since the tapping is carried out by other than
the investigating authorities—not only may not be used in
public proceedings, it may not even be mentioned. Above
all: what goes on in the "psyche" of the wiretapper? What
passes through the mind of a blameless civil servant who
is only doing his duty, who, we might say, is required to
do his duty (albeit reluctantly) by the exigencies of earn-
ing a living if not of obedience to orders? What does he
think when obliged to monitor a telephone conversation
between that unknown apartment dweller, whom we will
designate here the hawker of intimacies, and such an un-
usually nice, smart, virtually blameless person as Katharina Blum? Does he find himself in a state of moral or
sexual excitement, or both? Does he become indignant,
feel pity, or even derive some weird pleasure from a person nicknamed "the nun" being wounded in the depths
of her soul by hoarse and menacing propositions?

With all this happening in the foreground, even more is
going on in the background. What does a harmless wiretapper who is merely doing his job think when a certain
Lüding, who has been mentioned here from time to time,
calls up the editor in chief of the News and says something like: "S. right out, as of now, and B. in"? Naturally
Lüding is not being tapped because he has to be kept
under observation, but because of the threat that someone—blackmailer, politician, gangster, etc.—may call him
up. How is a blameless monitor to know that S. stands
for Sträubleder and B. for Blorna, and that readers of the
Sunday News will find nothing more about S. but a great

deal about B.? And yet—who is to know or even suspect this?—Blorna is an attorney of whom Lüding has the
highest opinion, one who time and again has proved
his skill at both the national and international level. When
elsewhere we speak of sources that "can never come together," all we are thinking of is the song about the prince
and the princess whose candle is blown out by the false
nun—and someone fell into rather deep water and
drowned.

And Mrs. Lüding tells her cook to call her husband's
secretary and find out what kind of dessert Lüding would
like on Sunday: crêpes with poppy seed? Strawberries
with ice cream *and* whipped cream, or with ice cream only
or with whipped cream only? Whereupon the secretary,
who would rather not disturb her boss but knows his
tastes yet on the other hand may merely want to cause
trouble, tells the cook with some asperity that she is convinced that this Sunday Mr. Lüding would prefer *crème
brûlée*. The cook, who of course also knows Lüding's
tastes, refuses to accept this, saying this is news to her and
is the secretary sure she is not confusing her own tastes
with those of Mr. Lüding, and would she kindly put her
through so she can talk to Mr. Lüding personally about
his dessert? Thereupon the secretary, who sometimes trav-
els with Mr. Lüding to conferences and has lunch or din-
ner with him at some Palace or Inter Hotel or other, claims
that when *she* is on a trip with him he invariably chooses
crème brûlée. The cook: but this Sunday he wasn't going
to be on a trip with her, the secretary, and mightn't Mr.
Lüding's choice of dessert depend on the society he happened to be in? Etc. Etc. Finally there was a long argument
about crêpes with poppy seed—and this entire conversation is recorded on tape at the taxpayer's expense! And
the person playing back the tape, who of course has to be
on the lookout for an anarchist code in which crêpes
might stand for hand grenades or strawberries and ice
cream for bombs—does he think: The problems some
people have! or: I wouldn't mind having such problems,

for his daughter might just have run away from home or his son have taken to hash, or the rent might have gone up again, and all this—these tape recordings—merely because someone once uttered a bomb threat against Lüding. And this is how some innocent civil servant or employee finally finds out what crêpes with poppy seed are—someone for whom even one crêpe would do as a main meal.

Too much is happening in the foreground, and we know nothing about what is happening in the background. If only one could replay the tapes! To discover at last the degree of intimacy, if any, between Miss Else Woltersheim and Konrad Beiters. How much does "friend" mean in terms of the relationship between these two? Does she call him Sweetheart, or Darling, or does she just say Konrad or Conny? What kind of verbal intimacies, if any, do they exchange? Does he sing to her over the phone—since he is known to have a good baritone voice, if not of concert at least of choral quality? Lieder? Serenades? Pop tunes? Operatic arias? Or might there even be crude itemizations of past or future intimacies? One would like to know, for most people, being denied reliable telepathic communication, reach for the phone, which they feel is more reliable. Do the authorities realize what they are asking of their employees in terms of the psyche? Let us assume that a temporarily suspect person of a vulgar nature, whose telephone is being officially tapped, calls up his equally vulgar sex partner of the moment. Since we live in a free country and may speak openly and frankly with one another, even over the phone, what sort of things may buzz in the ears of some moral, not to say moralistic, individual (regardless of sex) or come fluttering out of the tape? Can this be justified? Is there any provision for psychiatric treatment? What does the Union of Public Services, Transportation, and Communications say to *that*? There is concern for industrialists, anarchists, bank directors, bank robbers, and bank employees, but who is concerned about our national tape-security forces? Have the churches no com-

ment to make on this? Has the Bishops' Conference at
Fulda or the Executive Committee of German Catholics
no ideas on the subject? Why does the Pope keep silent?
Does no one realize all the things that assail innocent ears,
ranging from *crème brûlée* to hardest porn? We see young
people being encouraged to enter the civil service—
and to what are they exposed? To moral outcasts of the
telephone. Here at last we have an area where church
and trade union might cooperate. Surely it should be possible to plan at least some kind of educational program
for telephone monitors? History lessons on tape? That
shouldn't cost too much.

42

We now return contritely to the foreground, set to work
on the inescapable channeling process—and must begin
yet again with an explanation! We promised to let no more
blood flow, and we wish to stress that, with the death of
Mrs. Blum, Katharina's mother, this promise has not been
exactly broken. For this death, while not, of course, a normal one, was not a bloody murder. Mrs. Blum's death was
brought on by violence, true, but by unintentional violence. In any event—and this must be borne in mind—the
person responsible for her death had no intention of committing murder, manslaughter, or even mayhem. The person concerned—and for this there is not only evidence but
his own admission—was none other than Tötges, the very
man who himself came to such a bloody end as the result
of deliberate violence.

As early as Thursday, Tötges had inquired after and
obtained Mrs. Blum's address in Gemmelsbroich, but his
attempts to get into the hospital to see her were unsuccessful. He was informed by the doorman, by Sister Edelgard,
and by Dr. Heinen, that Mrs. Blum had just undergone a
serious but successful cancer operation and was urgently

in need of rest; that her recovery depended on not being exposed to any excitement whatever, and that an interview was out of the question. When reminded that, through her daughter's connection with Götten, Mrs. Blum was also a "public figure," the doctor countered with the remark that as far as he was concerned even public figures were first and foremost patients.

Now during this conversation Tötges had noticed that there were painters working in the building, and he later boasted to his colleagues that on Friday morning he succeeded, by using "the simplest trick in the book, the workman trick," that is, by getting hold of some overalls, a paint pot, and a paint brush, in getting in to see Mrs. Blum, for nothing was such a mine of information as a mother, even a sick one; he had, he said, confronted Mrs. Blum with the facts but wasn't quite sure whether she understood all he said, for the name Götten obviously didn't ring a bell with her and she had said: "Why did it have to end like this, why did it have to come to this?" out of which the *News* made: "It was bound to come to this, it was bound to end like this." Tötges accounted for the slight change in Mrs. Blum's statement by saying that as a reporter he was used to "helping simple people to express themselves more clearly."

43

It could not even be definitely established whether Tötges actually had got to see Mrs. Blum, or whether, in order to present the words quoted in the *News* as having been spoken by Katharina's mother in an interview, he had lied about or invented his visit as an example of his one-upmanship and efficiency as a reporter and to have something to boast about as well. Dr. Heinen, Sister Edelgard, a Spanish nurse called Huelva, a Portuguese cleaning woman called Puelco—all consider it out of the question that "this fellow should actually have had the nerve to do such a thing" (Dr. Heinen). Now there is no doubt that the visit to Katharina's mother—admitted although possibly invented—was of crucial importance, and the question naturally arises as to whether the hospital staff is simply denying what ought not to have happened, or whether Tötges, in order to authenticate the words of Katharina's mother, invented the visit. We must be scrupulously fair. There can be no doubt that it was *after* Katharina had arranged the interview with Tötges and *after* the *Sunday News* had published a further report by Tötges that she made herself the Bedouin costume in order to do some snooping in that very bar which the unfortunate Schönner had left "with some broad." So we must wait and see. One thing is certain, indeed confirmed, and that is that Dr. Heinen was surprised at the sudden death of his patient Maria Blum and that he could not "exclude the possibility of unforeseen influences, despite the lack of evidence." Innocent painters must not be saddled with the responsibility for this. The honor of the German craftsman must not be besmirched: neither Sister Edelgard nor the foreign ladies Huelva and Puelco can guarantee that all the painters—there were four of them, supplied by the firm of Merkens in Kuir—were in fact painters, and since all four were working in different parts of the building no one can be sure that someone in overalls and equipped with paint pot and brush did not sneak inside. The fact remains that Tötges *claimed* (the word "admitted" should not be used, since there is no actual evidence of his visit) to have seen Maria Blum and to have interviewed her, and Katharina knew of this claim. Furthermore, Mr. Merkens has admitted that of course not all of the four painters were present at the same time and that, *if* someone had wanted to sneak in, it would have been the simplest thing in the world. Dr. Heinen said later that he would bring a charge against the *News* for publishing the alleged remark of Katharina's mother and create a scandal for, if it was true, it was monstrous—but his threat remained as unex-

ecuted as the "punch in the jaw" with which Blorna had
threatened Sträubleder.

44

At about noon of that Saturday, February 23, 1974, the
Blornas, Miss Woltersheim, Konrad Beiters, and Katharina finally all got together at the Café Kloog in Kuir,
which was run by a nephew of the restaurant owner for
whom Katharina had sometimes worked in the past, in
the kitchen and as a waitress. Embraces were exchanged
and tears were shed, even by Mrs. Blorna. Needless to say,
the customers at the café were in Carnival mood, but the
proprietor, Erwin Kloog, an old and admiring friend of
Katharina's, put his own living room at the disposal of the
little group. From here, Blorna telephoned at once to
Hach, canceling the appointment for that afternoon in the
museum lobby. He told Hach that Katharina's mother had
died suddenly, probably as the result of a visit by Tötges
from the *News*. Hach was more subdued than he had
been that morning and asked Blorna to convey his personal sympathy to Katharina, who, he felt sure, bore him
no grudge, and indeed why should she? Of course, he was
at their disposal any time. Although he was very busy
right now with the interrogation of Götten he would certainly find the time; incidentally, so far nothing had shown
up in Götten's interrogation that could be damaging for
Katharina. Götten had spoken of her with great affection
and fairness. Permission for a visit, though, was not likely
to be forthcoming since they were not related and the
term "fiancée" would almost certainly prove too vague to
pass muster.

It looks very much as though Katharina was not exactly
in a state of collapse following the news of her mother's
death; it almost seems as though she was relieved. Of
course Katharina showed Dr. Heinen the edition of the

News in which the Tötges interview was mentioned and her mother was quoted, but she certainly did not share Dr. Heinen's indignation about the interview: on the contrary, she felt these people were murderers and character-assassins, and while naturally she despised them it was obviously the duty of that type of newspaper person to deprive the innocent of their honor, reputation, and health. Dr. Heinen, mistakenly assuming her to be a Marxist (probably he too had read the insinuations of Brettloh, Katharina's divorced husband, in the *News*), was taken aback by her detachment and asked her whether she considered it—this *modus operandi* of the *News*—to be a problem of the social structure. Katharina did not know what he meant, and shook her head.

She then followed Sister Edelgard to the mortuary, which she entered together with Miss Woltersheim. Katharina drew back the sheet from her mother's face with her own hands, said "Yes," and kissed her on the forehead; when Sister Edelgard suggested Katharina say a short prayer, she shook her head and said "No." She replaced the sheet over her mother's face, thanked the nun, and only on leaving the mortuary did she start to cry, at first softly, then harder, then uncontrollably. Perhaps she was also thinking of her dead father whom, when she was a child of six, she had also seen for the last time in a hospital mortuary. Else Woltersheim remembered, or rather noted, that she had never seen Katharina cry before, not even as a child when she had been unhappy at school or because of her wretched environment. Very courteously, almost with a smile, Katharina insisted on thanking everyone, including the foreign ladies Huelva and Puelco, for all they had done for her mother. She left the hospital quite composed, nor did she forget to ask the hospital administration to send a telegram to the prison where her brother Kurt was confined so he might be informed.

That was how she remained the whole afternoon and throughout the evening: composed. Although again and again she took out the two issues of the *News* and

confronted the Blornas, Else W., and Konrad B. with all
the details and her interpretation of them, even her attitude toward the *News* seemed to have changed. In today's
jargon: less emotional, more analytical. In this familiar
and sympathetic circle of friends, in Erwin Kloog's living room, she also spoke openly of her relationship to
Sträubleder: on one occasion he had brought her home
after an evening at the Blornas and, although she had
specifically and almost with revulsion told him not to, had
accompanied her as far as her front door and even into
her apartment by simply placing his foot in the door. And
then of course he had tried to make advances, probably
had felt insulted because she had not found him at all irresistible, and finally—it was already close to midnight—
had left. From then on he had positively persecuted
her, had kept coming back, sending flowers, writing letters, on a few occasions had even managed to get into her
apartment, and it was on one of those that he had simply
forced the ring on her. That was all. That was why she
had not admitted to his visits or revealed his name, because she had felt it would be impossible to explain to her
interrogators that there had been nothing, absolutely
nothing, not even a single kiss, between them. Who was
going to believe that she would resist a man like Sträubleder,
who was not only very well off but downright famous in
the political, economic, and academic world for his irresistible charm, almost like a movie star; and who was
going to believe of a woman like herself, a domestic, that
she would resist a movie star, and not for moral reasons
either but for reasons of taste? He had simply not had
the slightest attraction for her, and she regarded this whole
business of male visitors as the most horrible interfer-
ence in a sphere which she would not like to call intimate
since that would give the wrong impression and she had
not been even remotely intimate with Sträubleder—but
because he had got her into a situation that she could not
explain to anyone, let alone a team of investigators. In the
end, however—and here she laughed—she had felt grate-

ful to him in a way, for the key to his house had been a
big help to Ludwig, or at least the address, for—here she
laughed again—Ludwig would certainly have got in without a key, but of course the key made it easier, and she
had known too that the villa would be vacant during
Carnival, for only two days before Sträubleder had once
again made the worst possible nuisance of himself, positively forcing himself upon her and suggesting they spend
a Carnival weekend together at the house before he had
to leave for the conference at Bad B. in which he had
agreed to take part. Yes, Ludwig had told her the police
were looking for him, but he had merely said he was an
army deserter and about to leave the country, and—she
laughed for the third time—she had enjoyed personally
dispatching him into the heating duct and telling him
where the emergency exit was that led above ground at
the end of "Elegant Riverside Residences," at the corner
of Hochkeppel-Strasse. No, she had not thought that she
and Götten were being watched by the police, to her it
had been a kind of cops-and-robbers affair, and it wasn't
until next morning—Ludwig actually had left at six
o'clock—that she had come to realize how serious the
whole thing was. She registered relief that Götten had
been arrested: now, she said, he wouldn't be able to do
any more stupid things. She had been scared all the way
through, there had been something downright weird
about that Beizmenne.

45

At this juncture it must be noted that Saturday afternoon
and evening passed quite pleasantly, so pleasantly that
everyone—the Blornas, Else Woltersheim, and the strangely
silent Konrad Beiters—felt almost reassured. Finally there
was a general feeling—shared even by Katharina—that the
"situation had relaxed." Götten arrested, Katharina's

interrogation over, Katharina's mother released, albeit
sooner than expected, from great suffering; funeral ar-
rangements were already under way, all the necessary
documents in Kuir promised for the Monday before Lent,
an official having kindly declared his willingness to
issue them that day although it was a holiday. And finally
there was a certain consolation in the fact that the café
proprietor Erwin Kloog, who would not hear of accepting
payment for what had been consumed (i.e., coffee, li-
queurs, potato salad, wieners, and cake), said as they left:
"Chin up, Katie, not all of us here think badly of you." The
consolation inherent in these words was perhaps only
relative, for how much is "not all" worth? Still, the fact
remained that it was "not all." They agreed to drive to the
Blornas and spend the rest of the evening there. On arrival, Katharina was strictly forbidden to take a hand,
even her orderly one: she was on vacation and was told to
relax. It was Miss Woltersheim who made some sandwiches in the kitchen while Blorna and Beiters together
saw to the fire. And Katharina actually did let herself be
"spoiled for once." Everything was really very nice, and if
it had not been for a death and the arrest of a very dear
person they would certainly have had a little impromptu
dance in the small hours, for in spite of everything it was
Carnival.

Blorna was unable to dissuade Katharina from the
planned interview with Tötges. She remained calm and
smiling, and later, after the interview—some "interview"!—
Blorna felt his blood run cold at the recollection of the
cool determination with which Katharina had insisted on
the interview and how firmly she had declined his offer to
be present. And yet, later, he was not quite sure whether
Katharina had already decided on the murder that evening. It seemed to him much more likely that it had been
triggered by the *Sunday News*.

They bade each other a peaceful good night, again with
embraces, this time without tears, after listening to both
serious and popular music together and after both Katha-

rina and Else Woltersheim had told the others something about life in Gemmelsbroich and Kuir. It was barely
half-past ten when Katharina, Miss Woltersheim, and
Beiters parted from the Blornas with assurances of deep
regard and fellow-feeling, and the Blornas congratulated
themselves on having returned in time—in time to help
Katharina—after all. Over the ashes in the fireplace and a
bottle of wine, they discussed fresh vacation plans and the
character of their friend Sträubleder and his wife Maud.
When Blorna asked his wife to try not to use the phrase
"gentleman visitor" next time Sträubleder came, surely
she must see how hypersensitive the term had become,
Trude Blorna said: "It'll be a while before we see *him*
again."

46

We can vouch for Katharina having spent the rest of the
evening quietly. She tried on her Bedouin costume again,
went over some of the seams, and decided to use a white
handkerchief for a veil. They listened to the radio a while
longer, ate some cookies, and then took themselves off to
bed: Beiters going for the first time openly with Miss
Woltersheim into her bedroom, and Katharina making
herself comfortable on the sofa.

47

When Else Woltersheim and Konrad Beiters got up on
Sunday morning, they found the breakfast table nicely prepared, the coffee decanted into the Thermos jug, and Katharina, who was already having her breakfast and clearly
enjoying it, sitting at the living-room table reading the
Sunday News. What follows is not so much comment as

quotation. True, Katharina's "story" plus photo were no longer on the front page. This time the front page showed Ludwig Götten under the caption: "Intimate partner of Katharina Blum takes cover in industrialist's villa." The story itself was in greater detail than before and appeared on pages 7 to 9 with numerous pictures: Katharina as a First Communicant, her father as a returning soldier, the church in Gemmelsbroich, once again the Blorna villa; Katharina's mother at about forty, careworn, almost worn out, standing outside the cottage in Gemmelsbroich where they used to live, and finally a picture of the hospital where Katharina's mother had died Friday night. The text ran as follows:

A victim of her own daughter: so may we describe the mother of Katharina Blum, that shadowy figure who is still at large, Mrs. Blum not having survived the shock of being informed of her daughter's activities. While it is strange enough that, as her mother lay dying, the daughter should have been dancing at a ball in the tender embrace of a robber and murderer, it surely borders on the utmost perversity that she should have shed not a single tear at the news of her mother's death. Is this woman in truth merely "ice-cold and calculating"? The wife of one of her former employers, a respected country doctor, describes her as follows: "She behaved like a real little floozy. I had to let her go for the sake of my teenage sons, our patients, and my husband's reputation." Is it possible that Katharina B. was involved in the embezzling activities of the notorious Fehnern? (The *News* published a complete report of that case at the time.) Was her father a malingerer? Why did her brother turn to crime? Still awaiting explanation are her rapid rise in the world and her substantial income.

It has now been definitely established that Katharina Blum provided Götten, the man with blood on his hands, with the means of escape; she shamelessly abused the affection, confidence, and spontaneous generosity of a highly respected professional man and industrialist. Information is now in the hands of the *News* proving almost conclusively that her activities consisted not in *receiving* male visitors but in making unsolicited visits of her own in order to "case" the villa. Blum's "mystery drives" are no longer so mysterious. Without a shred of scruple she gambled the reputation of an honorable man, the happiness of his family, and his political career (on which the *News* has published frequent reports), indifferent to the feelings of a loyal wife and four children. It would appear that Blum had been instructed by a Leftist group to destroy S.'s career.

Do the police and the public prosecutor's office really intend to believe the infamous Götten in his protestations of Blum's complete innocence in the affair? As so often in the past, once again the *News* raises the question: Can it be denied that our methods of interrogation are too mild? Are we to continue to treat with humanity those who commit inhuman acts?

Beneath the photos of Blorna, Mrs. Blorna, and the villa:

It was in this house that Katharina Blum worked from seven A.M. to four-thirty P.M., on her own and unobserved, enjoying the full confidence of Dr. and Mrs. Blorna. What was going on here while the unsuspecting Blornas pursued their professions? Or were they not so unsuspecting after all? Their relationship with Blum is described as very cordial, almost familiar. Neighbors told reporters that it could almost be described as friendship. We will pass over certain insinuations since they are not relevant. Or are they? What was the role played by Mrs. Gertrud Blorna, known to this day in the records of a respected technical college as "Trude the Red"? How did Götten manage to escape from the Blum apartment although the police were on his heels? Who was familiar, down to the last detail, with the blueprints of the apartment complex known as "Elegant Riverside Residences"? Mrs. Blorna. Hertha Sch., sales clerk, and Claudia St., factory worker, made identical comments to the *News*:

"Those two, the way they danced together" (referring to
Blum and the outlaw Götten) "—it was as if they'd known
each other all their lives. That was no chance meeting, that
was a reunion."

48

When Beizmenne was later criticized by his colleagues for
having left Götten unmolested for almost forty-eight
hours, although his presence at the Sträubleder villa had
been known to the police since 11:30 P.M. Thursday, thus
risking another escape on the part of Götten, Beizmenne
laughed, saying that ever since midnight Thursday Götten
had had no further chance of escaping: the house was in
the woods but, by great good luck, was surrounded by
shooting blinds, "as if by watchtowers"; the Minister for
the Interior had been kept fully informed and had agreed
to all the measures taken; a helicopter, which of course did
not land within earshot, had put down a special detachment which was then deployed among the shooting blinds,
and the following morning the local police force had been
reinforced, very discreetly, by two dozen additional police
officers. The main objective had been to observe Götten's
attempts to make contact, and the success had justified
the risk. Five contacts had been spotted, and of course it
had first been necessary to pick up these five contacts and
search their homes before arresting Götten. The police
had waited to grab Götten until he had no further contacts to make and, out of either carelessness or bravado,
had felt so safe that it had been possible to observe him
from outside the villa.

Incidentally, there were certain important details for
which he had to thank reporters from the *News* as well as
the publishers of that paper and its affiliates that happened to have at their disposal more flexible and not always conventional methods of digging up information

that had remained hidden from the investigating authorities. For example, Miss Woltersheim had turned out to be just as much of an unknown quantity as Mrs. Blorna. Woltersheim had been born in 1930, the illegitimate child of a factory worker. The mother was still alive, and where do you suppose? In East Germany, and by no means against her will but voluntarily; she had frequently been invited to return to her native Kuir, where she owned a small house and an acre of land—the first time in 1945, again in 1952, yet again in 1961 shortly before the Berlin Wall went up. But she had refused—three times and all three times categorically. Of even greater interest was Woltersheim's father, a man called Lumm, likewise a factory worker and in addition a member of the then German Communist Party, and in 1932 he had emigrated to the Soviet Union, where he is said to have disappeared without trace. He—Beizmenne—supposed that this kind of missing person was not among those listed by the German Army as "missing."

49

There is always the possibility that certain relatively clear pointers toward a relationship between various events and actions will be misinterpreted or lost as mere hints; one further pointer should, therefore, be permitted: the *News*, which, of course, through its reporter Tötges was responsible for the unquestionably premature death of Katharina's mother, depicted Katharina in the *Sunday News* as being to blame for her mother's death and, moreover, accused her—more or less openly—of stealing Sträubleder's key to his country home! This point should be reemphasized, for one can never be sure; nor quite sure whether one has fully realized to what extent the *News* has slandered, lied, and distorted.

Let us take Blorna as an example of the *extent* to which

the *News* was able to affect comparatively rational people. We need hardly say that in the residential area where the Blornas lived no one bought the *Sunday News*. Reading tastes were loftier there. This explains how Blorna, who thought it was all over and was somewhat nervously awaiting the outcome of Katharina's conversation with Tötges, knew nothing about the article in the *Sunday News* until he called Miss Woltersheim. Miss Woltersheim, in turn, had taken it for granted that Blorna had already read the *Sunday News*. Now it is to be hoped that Blorna has been established as deeply and sincerely concerned for Katharina but also as a very level-headed person. On Miss Woltersheim now reading the relevant passages from the *Sunday News* aloud to him over the telephone, he could not—as they say—believe his ears. He asked her to read that again, after which he had not much choice but to believe it, and—as they say—he hit the roof. He shouted, roared, and rushed into the kitchen for an empty bottle, found one, ran off with it to the garage where, fortunately, he was intercepted by his wife and prevented from rigging up a Molotov cocktail that he intended to throw into the editorial offices of the *News,* to be followed by a second one into Sträubleder's town house. One must picture the scene: a man of forty-two, a university graduate, the object for the past seven years of Lüding's admiration and Sträubleder's respect for his sober, clear-headed negotiating abilities—and this on an international level, i.e., in Brazil, Saudi Arabia, and Northern Ireland, in other words not one of your provincial types but a thoroughgoing man of the world: *this* is the man who wanted to rig up a Molotov cocktail!

Mrs. Blorna dismissed this instantly as spontaneous petit-bourgeois romantic anarchism, "charmed away" his impulse the way one "charms away" disease or pain from some part of the body, went to the telephone herself and had Miss Woltersheim read the relevant passages to her. It cannot be denied that she, even she, turned somewhat pale, and she did something that may have been worse than any Molotov cocktail: she reached for the phone, called Lüding (who happened to be enjoying his strawberries *with* whipped cream *plus* vanilla ice cream), and simply said to him: "You bastard, you miserable little bastard!" She did not give her name, but it is safe to assume that all who knew the Blornas knew the voice of Mrs. Blorna, who was notorious for the asperity and deadly aim of her remarks. This, in her husband's opinion, was in turn going too far: he thought she was calling Sträubleder. Well, the result was one row after another, between the Blornas, and between the Blornas and other people, but since nobody was killed we must be allowed to pass over them. We mention these trifling, even if deliberate, consequences of the *Sunday News* reporting merely to point out how even well-educated, well-established people can be so carried away by their indignation that they consider resorting to violence of the crudest kind.

It is known that at about this time—around noon—Katharina, after spending an hour and a half, unrecognized, at the reporters' hangout, presumably gathering information on Tötges, left the place known as the "Golden Duck" and was waiting in her apartment for Tötges, who appeared some fifteen minutes later. We assume there is no more to be said concerning the "interview." The outcome is known. (See page 3.)

50

In order to check the truth of the statement made by the Gemmelsbroich pastor—a statement that had surprised *everyone* involved—that Katharina's father had been a Communist in disguise, Blorna drove out to the village, where he spent a day. First of all: the pastor confirmed his statement, saying that the *News* had quoted him correctly and word for word, no, he could offer no proof of his claim nor did he want to, he even said he did not *need* to, he could still rely on his sense of smell and he had simply smelled that Blum was a Communist. When asked to define his sense of smell he refused, nor was he very helpful when Blorna then asked him kindly to explain, if he could not define his sense of smell, *what* the smell of a Communist was like, *how* a Communist smelled, and at this point—it has to be said—the pastor became quite rude, asked Blorna whether he was a Catholic and, when Blorna said yes, reminded him of his duty to be obedient, which Blorna did not understand. From then on, he ran into difficulties over his inquiries concerning the Blums, who did not appear to have been especially popular; he heard bad things about Katharina's deceased mother, who had indeed finished *one* bottle of sacramental wine in the sacristy with the help of the verger (since dismissed); he heard bad things about Katharina's brother, who had been a regular nuisance, but the only words of Katharina's father to substantiate his Communism were a remark he made in 1949 to Scheumel, a farmer, in one of the seven village taverns, and this was supposed to have been: "There are worse things than Socialism." That was all he could glean. The only result for Blorna was that, at the conclusion of his inquiries in the village, he was himself described, if not precisely abused, as a Communist, and that came (something he found particularly painful) from a woman who until then had been quite helpful and had even displayed a certain sympathy toward him: the retired schoolteacher Elma Zubringer who, as he said good-bye, gave him a mocking smile, even a bit of a wink, saying: "Why don't you admit that you're one of them too—and your wife most of all?"

51

Unfortunately we cannot ignore one or two acts of violence that occurred while Blorna was preparing for the trial of

THE LOST HONOR OF KATHARINA BLUM

Katharina. His greatest mistake was in acceding to Katharina's request to take over Götten's defense as well, and in repeatedly trying to obtain permission for the two to visit each other, insisting that they were engaged. It was, he maintained, in the course of that very evening, February 20, and of the ensuing night that the engagement had taken place. Etc. Etc. It is not hard to imagine the kind of thing the *News* wrote about him, about Götten and Katharina, about Mrs. Blorna. We do not intend to cite each instance here. Certain infringements of or departures from the level are to be undertaken only when necessary, and here they are not necessary because by this time the reader must know what to expect from the *News*. The rumor was being circulated that Blorna wanted a divorce, a rumor without a grain of truth to it but which nevertheless sowed the seeds of mistrust between husband and wife. It was claimed that he was in financial straits, which was bad because it was true. The fact was that he had somewhat overextended himself in assuming a kind of custodianship for Katharina's apartment, which was almost impossible to rent or sell because it was considered "bloodstained." Anyway, it dropped in value, yet Blorna had to continue the payments for amortization, interest, etc., in unreduced amounts. In fact there was already some indication that Haftex, the owners of "Elegant Riverside Residences," were considering suing Katharina Blum for damages, claiming that she had impaired the rental, commercial, and social value of their apartment complex. We see then: trouble, quite a lot of trouble. An application to the courts for permission to dismiss Mrs. Blorna from the architectural firm on grounds of breach of confidence (i.e., familiarizing Katharina with the substructure of the apartment complex) was turned down, but nobody is sure which way the appeal courts will decide. One more thing: the Blornas have already got rid of their second car, and recently there was a picture in the *News* of the Blorna limousine, which really is rather elegant, over the caption: "When will the 'red' attorney have to switch to the average man's car?"

52

Need we say that Blorna's association with Lüsträ has been affected if not dissolved? The only matters still under discussion now are the "winding up" of certain transactions. However, he was recently informed by Sträubleder over the telephone: "We're not going to let you and Trude starve," and what surprised Blorna in this was Sträubleder's inclusion of Trude. He still acts on behalf of Lüsträ and Haftex but no longer at the international or even the national level, only rarely at the regional and mostly at the local level. In other words, he has to grapple with petty defaulters and troublemakers who submit claims for the promised marble paneling when the walls have been faced with mere green slate; or types who, when they have been promised three coats of enamel on their bathroom doors, scrape off the paint with a knife and hire experts to confirm that there are only two coats. Then there are the dripping faucets and defective garbage disposals used as a pretext for withholding contractual payments—this is the kind of case now being dumped in his lap, whereas he used to be flying continually, if not continuously, between Buenos Aires and Persepolis to take part in plans for major projects. In the army this is known as a demotion, a process usually associated with some degree of humiliation. Result: no stomach ulcers yet, but Blorna's stomach is beginning to complain.

It was unfortunate that he made his own inquiries in Kohlforstenheim with a view to finding out from the local chief of police whether the key had been on the inside or the outside of the door at the time of Götten's arrest, or whether there had been any sign of Götten having broken in. Why bother, now that the inquiries have all been completed? This—there is no denying—is no way to cure stomach ulcers, for all that Police Chief Hermanns was very nice to him, and yet, far from accusing him of Communism, he did strongly urge him not to interfere. There is one consolation for Blorna: his wife is being nicer to him all the time, and although she still has a sharp tongue she now reserves it for use against others (although not against all others) instead of against him. So far the only obstacle to her plan of selling the villa and buying Katharina's apartment for themselves is the size of the apartment: it is too small, for Blorna wants to give up his town office and wind up any outstanding business at home. Blorna, who used to be known as liberal-minded and a *bon vivant,* a popular, jovial colleague who gave wonderful parties, is beginning to take on the air of an ascetic and to neglect his appearance, to which he had always attached great importance; and because he is *genuinely* neglecting it, not just as a fad, some of his colleagues are even saying that he is overlooking the most basic personal hygiene and no longer smells as he should. Hence there is little reason to hope for a new career for him, the fact being (nothing, nothing whatever, must be withheld) that his body no longer smells as it used to, i.e., like that of a man who every morning jumps into the shower and uses plenty of soap, deodorant, and toilet water. In short: a considerable change is taking place in him. His friends—he still has a few, among them Hach, with whom he happens to be professionally involved in the Götten and Blum cases—are seriously concerned, especially since his aggressions—e.g., vis-à-vis the *News,* which still remembers him from time to time with short items—no longer explode but are quite obviously being swallowed. His friends' concern is such that they have asked Trude Blorna to check discreetly whether Blorna is acquiring any weapons or concocting explosives, for the murdered Tötges has a successor who, under the name of Eginhard Templer, is carrying on a kind of continuation of Tötges; this Templer managed to photograph Blorna just as the latter was entering a pawnshop; then, by photographing through the window, he was able to offer readers of the *News* a view of Blorna negotiating with the pawnbroker: under discussion was the loan value of a ring being scrutinized by the pawnbroker through a jeweler's loupe. Caption: "Have the 'red' sources really dried up, or is someone faking financial distress?"

53

Blorna's chief concern is to persuade Katharina to testify at the actual trial that she did not make the decision to take revenge on Tötges until the Sunday morning, and that her intention had been not to kill him but to scare him off. She was to say that, although on the Saturday, when she invited Tötges to an interview, she had meant to tell him what she thought of him in no uncertain terms and to point out what he had done to her life and her mother's life, she had not wanted to kill him even on the Sunday, even after reading the article in the *Sunday News*. He felt it was imperative to avoid the impression that Katharina had planned the murder for several days and had proceeded according to plan. Although she claims to have *thought about* murder on Thursday after reading the first article, he tried to make her realize that many people—including himself—occasionally do think about murder but that one must distinguish between thinking about murder and planning a murder.

Another thing worrying Blorna is that Katharina is still showing no signs of remorse, which means that she will not be able to show any in court. She is not at all depressed: on the contrary, she seems quite happy because she is living "under the same conditions as my dear Ludwig." She is considered a model prisoner, works in the kitchen but, if the opening of the trial is further delayed, is to be transferred to the commissary where, however (so one hears), she is most unenthusiastically awaited: there is dismay on the part of both administration and inmates at the reputation for integrity that precedes her, and the pros-

pect of Katharina spending her entire prison term working
within the commissary system (it is predicted that a sentence of fifteen years will be asked for and that she will
get eight to ten) is spreading alarm through every prison
in the country. Thus we see that integrity, combined with
intelligent organizing ability, is not desired anywhere, not
even in prisons, and not even by the administration.

54

As Hach informed Blorna in confidence, the murder
charge against Götten is not likely to stand up and will
therefore be dropped. The fact that he not only deserted
from the army but also acted to the considerable detri-
ment (both moral and material) of this hallowed institu-
tion is regarded as proven. His crime was not bank
robbery but the total cleaning out of a safe that had contained the pay for two regiments as well as substantial
cash reserves; also falsifying the accounts and theft of a
weapon. Well, a sentence of eight to ten years is expected
for him too. This means that when released he would be
about thirty-four and Katharina about thirty-five, and
she really does have plans for the future: she calculates
that by the time she is released interest will have increased
her capital substantially, and when the time comes she
intends to open, "somewhere, not here of course," a "restaurant with outside catering service." Permission to consider herself Götten's fiancée will probably be decided at
the highest, not merely a higher, level. The relevant ap-
plications have been submitted and are already on their
long march from one department to another. Incidentally,
the telephone contacts made by Götten from Sträubleder's
country house were all to members of the army or their
wives, including officers and officers' wives. A scandal of
moderate dimensions is predicted.

55

While Katharina, restricted only in her freedom, is looking almost untroubled to the future, Else Woltersheim is
on the way to a state of steadily increasing bitterness. She
was extremely upset at the defamation of her mother and
her deceased father, who is regarded as a victim of Stalin-
ism. There are indications in Else Woltersheim of intensi-
fied antisocial tendencies which not even Konrad Beiters
is able to alleviate. Since Else is now specializing more and
more in cold buffets, i.e., in organizing, supplying, and
supervising them, her aggressiveness is being increasingly
directed at the guests, whether foreign or domestic journalists, industrialists, trade-union officials, bankers, or
junior executives. "Sometimes," she told Blorna not long
ago, "I have to force myself not to throw a bowl of potato
salad over the tuxedo of some moron or a plate of smoked
salmon down the cleavage of some stupid cow, just to see
them shudder for once. Try and imagine the picture from
our side: how they stand there with their mouths wide
open and their tongues hanging out and how of course
they all make a dash for the caviar canapés—and there
are some who I know are millionaires, or the wives of
millionaires, who even stuff their pockets and purses with
cigarettes and matches and petits fours. Soon they'll be
bringing along plastic containers to carry away the coffee—and all that, every bit of it, is being paid for one way
or another out of our taxes. There are characters who go
without breakfast or lunch so they can fall like vultures
on a cold buffet—not that I mean to insult vultures."

56

So far we know of only one instance of an actual exchange
of blows, one which unfortunately aroused a good deal of

public attention. It was at the preview of the exhibition of the work of the painter Frederick Le Boche, whose patron Blorna is considered to be, that Blorna and Sträubleder came face-to-face again for the first time. As Sträubleder approached him with a broad grin, Blorna did not hold out his hand, but this did not prevent Sträubleder from grabbing it and whispering: "For God's sake, don't take it all so seriously! We're not going to let you and Trude go to the dogs—you're the one who's doing that." Well, if we are to be honest we have regretfully to report that at this moment Blorna did punch Sträubleder in the jaw. Without further ado, so that it may be forgotten without further ado: blood flowed, from Sträubleder's nose; according to private estimates, some four to seven drops but, what was worse: although Sträubleder backed away he did say: "I forgive you, I forgive you everything—considering your emotional state." And so it was that this remark apparently maddened Blorna, provoking something described by witnesses as a "scuffle," and, as is usually the case when the Sträubleders and Blornas of this world show themselves in public, a *News* photographer by the name of Kottensehl (successor to the murdered Schönner) was present, and we can hardly be shocked at the *News* (its nature being now known) for publishing the photograph of this scuffle under the heading: "Conservative politician assaulted by Leftist attorney." Not until the following morning, of course.

At the exhibition there was furthermore a confrontation between Maud Sträubleder and Trude Blorna. Maud Sträubleder said to Trude Blorna: "I do sympathize with you so, Trude dear," whereupon Trude B. said to Maud S.: "You can put your sympathy right back in the fridge where you keep all the rest of your feelings." Upon Maud again offering her forgiveness, indulgence, pity, indeed almost love, with the words: "Nothing, nothing, not even your destructive remarks, can lessen my sympathy," Trude B. replied in words that cannot be repeated here, only noted; ladylike is not the way to describe the words in

which Trude B. hinted at Sträubleder's numerous advances
to her and, among other things—thus violating the professional secrecy to which even the wife of an attorney is
bound—alluded to the ring, the letters, and key which
"your consistently rejected suitor left behind in a certain
apartment." At this point the squabbling ladies were
parted by Frederick Le Boche, who with great presence of
mind had seized upon the chance to catch Sträubleder's
blood on a piece of blotting paper and had converted it
into what he called "a specimen of instant art." This he
entitled "End of a Long Friendship," signed, and gave not
to Sträubleder but to Blorna, saying: "Here's something
you can peddle to help you out of a hole." From this oc-
currence plus the preceding acts of violence it should be
possible to deduce that Art still has a social function.

57

It is indeed deplorable that here, as we approach the conclusion, there should be so little harmony to report and
but slight hope of any in the future. The outcome has been
not integration but confrontation. Naturally the question
must arise: *Why?* Here is a young woman, cheerfully, almost gaily, going off to a harmless little private dance, and
four days later she becomes (since this is merely a report,
not a judgment, we will confine ourselves to facts) a mur-
deress, and this, if we examine the matter closely, because
of newspaper reports. We see quarrels and tensions and
finally scuffles arising between two men who have been
friends for a very, very long time. Pointed remarks made
by their wives. Rejected sympathy, in fact rejected love.
Highly unpleasant developments. A genial, broad-minded
man, who loves life, travel, luxury, neglects himself so
seriously that he emits body odor! He has even been
found to have bad breath. He puts his house up for sale,
he goes to the pawnbroker. His wife is looking around

"for another job" since she is convinced that her firm's second application for dismissal will go against her; she is even prepared—this talented woman is prepared—to work as little better than a sales clerk (with the title "Interior Decorating Consultant") for one of the large furniture outfits, but there she is told "that the circles in which we are accustomed to do business are precisely those, Madam, where you have made enemies."

In short: things do not look good. Hach, the public prosecutor, has already been whispering to friends something that he has not yet had the courage to tell Blorna: that Blorna may be turned down as defense counsel on grounds of his undue involvement. What will happen, how will it end? What will happen to Blorna if he can no longer visit Katharina and—it has to come out!—hold hands with her? There is no doubt about it: he loves her, she does not love him, and he hasn't a hope in the world, since everything, everything, belongs to her "dear Ludwig"! And we must add that this "holding hands" is a purely one-sided affair, for all it consists of is that, when Katharina passes files or notes or papers across to him, he places his hands on hers for longer—perhaps three, four, at most five tenths of a second longer—than is customary. How in the world are we to bring about harmony here, when not even his strong attachment to Katharina prompts him to, let us say, wash a bit more often? Not even the fact that he, he alone, discovered the origin of the murder weapon—where Beizmenne, Moeding, and their assistants had failed—was any comfort to him. Perhaps it is too much to say "discovered": what actually happened was that Konrad Beiters voluntarily admitted to having once been a Nazi and that this alone explained why so far no one had paid any attention to him. It was true, he had been Party leader in Kuir and at the time had been able to do something for Miss Woltersheim's mother, and, well, the pistol was an old service one that he had kept hidden but stupidly enough occasionally shown to Else and Katharina; the three of them had once even gone out into the woods for some target practice; Katharina had turned out to be a good shot and had told him that as a girl she had worked as a waitress at Rifle Club meetings and had sometimes been allowed to fire a few rounds. Well, on the Saturday evening Katharina had asked him for the key to his apartment, saying she hoped he would understand, she just wanted to be alone for a while, her own apartment was dead for her, dead—yet that Saturday night she had stayed with Else so she must have picked up the pistol from his apartment on the Sunday, it must have been after breakfast and after reading the *Sunday News,* when she had driven off in her Bedouin costume to that reporters' hangout.

58

But finally we do have something reasonably cheerful to report: Katharina told Blorna the whole story; she also told him how she had spent the six or seven hours between the murder and her appearance at Moeding's home. We are in the fortunate position of being able to quote. Fortunately, this account can be quoted verbatim, Katharina having written it all down and given Blorna permission to use it at the trial.

"The only reason I went to that reporters' bar was to have a look at him. I wanted to know what that kind of man looked like, what his movements were like, how he talked, drank, danced—that man who had destroyed my life. Yes, I did go first to Konrad's apartment to pick up the pistol, I even loaded it myself. I had asked him to show me how, that time we did some target practice in the woods.

"I waited in the bar for an hour and a half, maybe two hours, but he didn't show up. I had decided that, if he was too awful, I wouldn't even go to the interview, and it's true—if I had seen him before I wouldn't have gone. But he never came to the bar. To avoid being pestered, I asked the landlord—his name is Peter Kraffluhn, I know him from the extra jobs I take on, where he sometimes helps out as head waiter—I asked him to let me help serve behind the bar. Of course Peter knew what the *News* had been saying about me, he had promised to give me the high sign if Tötges turned up. Seeing it was Carnival, I didn't mind being asked to dance a few times, but when Tötges failed to show up I must say I got very nervous, I didn't want to meet with him cold.

"So at noon I drove home, and I felt terrible in that stained and soiled apartment. I only had to wait a few minutes before the bell rang, just enough time to release the safety catch on the pistol and slip it into my handbag ready to pull out. And then the bell rang, and there he was outside the door when I opened it, and here I'd been thinking he had pressed it downstairs and I would have a few extra minutes, but he had already come up in the elevator, and there he was, standing right in front of me, and it was a shock. Well, I could see right away what a bastard he was, a real bastard. And good-looking, too. What people call good-looking. Anyway, you've seen his pictures. He said: 'Well, Blumikins, what'll we do now, you and me?' I didn't say a word, just stepped back into the living room, and he followed me in, saying: 'Why do you look at me like that, Blumikins, as if you're scared out of your wits? How about us having a bang for a start?' Well, by this time I had my hand in my purse, and as he went for my dress I thought: 'Bang, if that's what you want,' and I pulled out the pistol and shot him then and there. Twice, three times, four times—I don't remember exactly. The police report will tell you how many times. Now I don't want you to think this was something new for me, a man going for my dress—when you've worked in other people's homes ever since you were fourteen, and even earlier, you're used to that. But *this* fellow—and then 'a bang'! and I thought: O.K., bang away. Of course he hadn't counted on that, and for a split second he looked at me in amazement, like in the movies when someone gets shot out of a clear blue sky. Then he fell to the floor, and I think he was dead. I threw the pistol down beside him and fled, down in the elevator and back to the bar, and Peter was astonished, since I'd been gone hardly half an hour. I went on working at the bar but I didn't dance any more, and all the time I was thinking, 'It can't be true,' but I knew it was true. And now and again Peter would come up and say: 'He's not going to show today, that boy friend of yours,' and I would say: 'Doesn't look like it.' And behave as if I didn't care. Until four o'clock I poured schnapps and drew beer and opened champagne bottles and served snacks. Then I left, without saying good-bye to Peter. First I went into a church next door and sat there for maybe half an hour thinking about my mother and the wretched miserable life she had had, and about my father too, who was always grumbling, always always, and cursing the government and the church and the civil service, and officers and everything, but whenever he had anything to do with any of them he would crawl, almost whimper, as he groveled. And I thought about my husband, Brettloh, and about those rotten lies he told Tötges, and of course about my brother, who was forever after my money the minute I'd earned a few marks and managed to squeeze it out of me for some nonsense or other, like clothes or motorbikes or gambling, and of course about the pastor, who in school always used to call me 'our pink Katie,' and I didn't know what he meant, and the whole class would laugh because then I really would turn pink. Yes. And of course about Ludwig. Then I left the church and went to the nearest movie, and left the movie again, and went into another church, because on that Carnival Sunday it was the only place where a person could find a bit of peace. And of course I thought about the dead man back there in my apartment. Without remorse, without regret. He had wanted a bang, hadn't he, and I'd banged, hadn't I? And for a moment I thought it was the fellow who used to ring me up at night and who had pestered

poor Else too. I thought: that's his voice all right, and I
wanted to let him rattle on for a bit, to be quite sure, but
what good would that have done me? And then I suddenly
longed for some strong coffee and went to the Café Bekering, not to the restaurant but to the kitchen, because I
knew Käthe Bekering, the owner's wife, from home-ec
school. Käthe was very kind to me, although she was
pretty busy. She gave me a cup of her own coffee, the kind
Grandma used to make by pouring boiling water onto the
ground coffee. But then she began talking about that stuff
in the *News*, quite nicely yet somehow in a way that made
me feel she believed at least a bit of it—and anyway how
are people to know that it's all lies? I tried to explain to
her, but she didn't understand, she just winked at me and
said, 'So you really love this fellow?' and I said, 'Yes.' And
then I thanked her for the coffee, and when I got outside
I took a cab and drove to see Moeding, the police officer
who had been so nice to me before."

CLICK ON A CLASSIC
www.penguinclassics.com
The world's greatest literature at your fingertips

Constantly updated information on over 1600 titles, from
Icelandic sagas to ancient Indian epics, Russian drama to
Italian romance, American greats to African masterpieces

•

The latest news on recent additions to the list, updated
editions and specially commissioned translations

•

Original scholarly essays by leading writers: Elaine Showalter
on Zola, Laurie R King on Arthur Conan Doyle, Frank
Kermode on Shakespeare, Lisa Appignanesi on Tolstoy

•

A wealth of background material, including biographies
of every classic author from Aristotle to Zamyatin, plot
synopses, readers' and teachers' guides, useful web links

•

Online desk and examination copy assistance for academics

•

Trivia quizzes, competitions, giveaways, news on
forthcoming screen adaptations

•

eBooks available to download

THE STORY OF PENGUIN CLASSICS

Before 1946 . . . "Classics" are mainly the domain of academics and students; readable editions for everyone else are almost unheard of. This all changes when a little-known classicist, E. V. Rieu, presents Penguin founder Allen Lane with the translation of Homer's *Odyssey* that he has been working on in his spare time.

1946 Penguin Classics debuts with *The Odyssey*, which promptly sells three million copies. Suddenly, classics are no longer for the privileged few.

1950s Rieu, now series editor, turns to professional writers for the best modern, readable translations, including Dorothy L. Sayers's *Inferno* and Robert Graves's unexpurgated *Twelve Caesars*.

1960s The Classics are given the distinctive black covers that have remained a constant throughout the life of the series. Rieu retires in 1964, hailing the Penguin Classics list as "the greatest educative force of the twentieth century."

1970s A new generation of translators swells the Penguin Classics ranks, introducing readers of English to classics of world literature from more than twenty languages. The list grows to encompass more history, philosophy, science, religion, and politics.

1980s The Penguin American Library launches with titles such as *Uncle Tom's Cabin* and joins forces with Penguin Classics to provide the most comprehensive library of world literature available from any paperback publisher.

1990s The launch of Penguin Audiobooks brings the classics to a listening audience for the first time, and in 1999 the worldwide launch of the Penguin Classics Web site extends their reach to the global online community.

The 21st Century Penguin Classics are completely redesigned for the first time in nearly twenty years. This world-famous series now consists of more than 1,300 titles, making the widest range of the best books ever written available to millions—and constantly redefining what makes a "classic."

The Odyssey continues . . .

The best books ever written

PENGUIN CLASSICS

SINCE 1946